DISORDERLY CONDUCT

College Edition

The Disorderly Conduct series is satirical erotica written for a mature audience 18 or older.

By: Jade Greene
Editing By: Hope Marian

WingSpan Press

Published in the United States and the United Kingdom

by WingSpan Press, Livermore, CA

The WingSpan name, logo and colophon are the trademarks of WingSpan Publishing.

ISBN 978-1-63683-036-0 (pbk.)
ISBN 978-1-63683-971-4 (ebk.)

First edition 2022

Printed in the United States of America

www.wingspanpress.com

Dedication And Thanks

I want to dedicate this novel to a few incredible people who inspired it. When I was an undergrad, I had to reconcile what it meant to be an all-women's college student, pageant girl and party animal. I had the privilege to meet fun-loving people and hook up with hotties while finding my own identity.

I specifically want to thank Huey Mack, Mike, and Jon Kilmer for producing the anthem music for most millennials' college experiences. I learned from the best and the hottest. Not one for drama, I just wanted to spend my 20s engulfed in debauchery, and you three inspired me to do so.

By embracing my inner frat boy, I made lasting friendships that I am still lucky enough to have to this day. Thank you to one of my best friends Spencer who helped make this possible and for being there at the beginning of my erotica writing journey. I also want to thank all my college friends who provided ample laughter and adventures - Maddy, Judy, Lauren, Mike, Norma, and Nikki.

You guys are the most genuine people I've ever met and gave me the liveliest experience while we were all in college. Lastly, I want to thank my late friend Meg who left us too soon, only a few years after graduation.

Contents

CHAPTER 1

Back and Better

It was 2011, the first weekend after the fall semester started and my junior year attending college in Wilmington, Delaware. Although my heart was demolished in the summer prior by my high school sweetheart, I was cheered up immediately the day after. I won a beauty and scholarship pageant and was officially the reigning Miss Delaware. Once I went back to school, my head was inflated, and my ego burning. Looking back, I was somewhat of an obnoxious tool.

Being "crowned" so recently, I wanted to make sure I stuck to a routine that allowed time for both work and play. Throughout the weekdays, I stayed incredibly disciplined, balancing my schedule between appearances, studying, and working out. I didn't drink much since I consistently had a low tolerance. Being 5'2 and 105 pounds, drinking was never a good idea. Therefore, I rationalized that smoking was a better vice to have.

I didn't care what others thought about my habits. I could validate myself, and I just wanted success and happiness like everyone else. The haze of adolescence had lifted, and I was more than happy to enjoy the view.

By my third year of college, the environment became like a familiar abode. Outside the 12th floor window of a new "friend's" apartment, a siren rudely interrupted the quiet of the night.

"I have to go." I woke up and said coldly.

"You sure you don't want to stay the night? It's pretty late, and I cook a great breakfast!" He responded with the most enthusiasm he could give at 2 am.

This was just a part of a new unhealthy routine, a part of the game that I enjoyed playing. Although it was a frowned upon lifestyle, I was content being promiscuous. Slowly I slid out of bed, gathered my things, and gracefully exited without looking back. Absolutely exhausted, I walked to my car and pulled out my stash of weed. I noticed an extra wrap under my car seat and decided it would be a good time to smoke. On my way back to school, I lit a fat juicy blunt. I didn't care.

The feeling of smoking brought me down from a night of excitement and playtime. Driving past the Hott Chocolate Café and the river were sights to see. Here I was, a former bullied, straight edge nerd who now lived the fast-paced East Coast city life. I was a stoner beauty queen with a posse of human sex toys. I could do whatever, whenever, and whoever I wanted. I finally arrived back in my bed by 3 am. The feeling of my down comforter was fantastic. I also saved up some money to rent my whole dorm instead of having a roommate. Oh yes, this year was going to be my best.

It was 6 am and the alarm sounded like a dying animal. Immediately, I regretted registering for a Saturday computer science class. Although I empathized with my professor, an overly excitable woman who was passionate about everything she did. Like every day, I got up, walked to a good spot, and smoked a bowl before class. Unlike the common stereotypes of potheads, weed made me feel clear. Strangely, it gave me a desire to work out and pursue athletic goals. It destroyed my test anxiety and, to others' dismay, motivated me. I returned to campus just in time to catch breakfast. I ate quickly and took my coffee to go. Walking to class, I saw my friend Madison. Madison was a sweetheart and always supported me, no matter how outrageous my behavior became.

"Arie! What's up? How was your Friday?" She greeted me warmly.

"It was alright, same old. Still trying to see if any of these gents can capture me but no success, it seems," I replied casually yet structured.

"What are you, a Pokémon?" She asked humorously. I died laughing.

We walked down to the science building from the uphill cafeteria talking shit, smoking cigarettes, and chatting away. It was empowering, uplifting, and refreshing to be surrounded by women with innovative minds and similar interests. When I chose a college in high school, I knew I wanted to attend an urban all-women's university. Lucky for me, Delaware Women's University, DWU, was the right choice. Women at my school were driven, unique, and genuine. Even those rare few who didn't get along didn't cause drama. They simply avoided one another.

The class ended, and everyone exited the room to carry on with their weekends. My phone buzzed, and it was a text from the most attractive frat boy I knew... Anthony. He was tall, dark haired, easy on the eyes, and an athletic young specimen of a Jewish American male. His smile was visually magnetic.

I met him the year before, during my sophomore year of college, on a freezing day. The bus to work was overcrowded, which meant I had nowhere to sit, and he offered me a seat right next to him. On that ride, we found out we were both enthusiastic smokers and athletes. I ran and he played baseball at DMU, the formerly all-men's university down the road, so it was easy to make conversation with him. I was undeniably drawn to him. We smoked weed together a few times that year, but sexually misbehaving was prevented by my controlling boyfriend. I texted him back.

Anthony: Hey, how was your summer? Did you move back into your dorms yet?

Me: Well, hello there, handsome. I hope you had a fun summer. Mine went well, thanks for asking.

Me: Wellllll I'm single and won Miss Delaware :-P

Anthony: Oh shit! That's sick Arie. Congratulations.

Me: Tyvm cutie …. How about we celebrate this weekend? ;-)

Anthony: I'm so down.

Done and done. I was so excited to get back on my game, show off, and of course, get laid. In a way, my friends and I were much like frat boys. It was not unusual for me to lead my sexy pack of beautiful minions to the formerly all-male university the next mile over. We were unstoppable.

Anthony: Let me know what's up!

Me: Alright, I know my girl is having a party over at her house in Newark next weekend

Anthony: Sounds good. I can bring some of my boys too if you want :-P

Me: Mmmm yes, please do ☺ <3

"Sweet," I thought. I already made plans for my second weekend of junior year. "And to think, with the hottest guy at our brother school," my thoughts were racing, and I decided now would be a good time to find my group of friends and strategize. There was only one cardinal rule and two goals on our group rendezvous. The rule was to respect the group more than the men, meaning that if one friend wanted a guy (unless a threesome was established as acceptable), all other ladies in our group actively backed off. The two goals were to get numbers and get laid. It was simple and worked for us because we had established the process, and there were never any issues among my wonderful crew.

I was thrilled to start the weekend right. My best friend Kathy texted me and wanted to hang out immediately. Since I was still living with my mom out of state, I hadn't seen her all summer. After twenty minutes she confirmed that she had arrived with "supplies".

Kathy: Arieeeeeeeeeeeeeeeeeeee. I'm here; let's smoke.

Me: Yessssss, my love. I concur with your suggestion!

I grabbed my handbag and a cardigan, just in case

we stayed out late. Hastily, I locked my door and ran down the stairs. A few familiar faces passed, cheerfully greeting me and I made my way out the double glass front doors. Kathy welcomed me back into her life blasting dubstep and wearing her original 1970s gold rimmed Ray Bans in her special silver edition chromed out Jeep. She was an intellectual and blonde badass. Her parents weren't millionaires, but they had no problem spoiling her. It was awesome that she had the coolest parents of the group who let us smoke in the house.

I waved at her as I rushed to the front passenger seat. To my surprise, my other closest friend Deedee occupied it. I knocked aggressively on her window which prompted me losing it and jumping up and down. Still laughing, I opened the back seat door and hopped in. Hugs and positive vibes were shared the instant I closed the door.

"Thank God for this school of beautiful bitches and these beautiful buds of cannabis!" Kathy cheered.

"Alright! The crew is complete again!" Deedee hollered. We were blissfully forming an airspace entirely composed of sinful energy. I pulled out my meager stash to share. Deedee gave a nod of approval after inspecting the quality carefully.

"Hell yeah, ladies!!! Let's roll this shit up, discuss plans, and get baked like a cake!" I responded.

Seeing my friends after a long miserable summer alone in my home state felt like a family reunion. We were a quirky group and secretly called ourselves the *Bad Girls Club of DWU*. It had members of all classes, but we were the proud class of 2013. Kathy was beautiful with golden hair and natural honey highlights, a nice body, and totally was the ringleader.

Deedee was our attractive black-haired, chocolate-skinned athletic baddie and the elected muscle of the group. She was dating the Greek bombshell, Angie. We also had Crystal, who was a black-haired, medium-dark-skinned fireball and daughter of the Delaware governor. Kendra was the ultimate female player of the crew. Jenny was our softie, a sweetie who suffered from frequent medical issues but loved to party. Aside from Jenny and Deedee, the rest of us were pansexual or bisexual. I considered myself pan, but I didn't care if someone called me bi. I had better luck with men than women as per my preference for instant gratification.

We drove along the main road downtown and finally made it into our usual designated "blunt ride" neighborhood. Wilmington was an odd city. A block away from the impoverished lived the wealthy... and Crystal. Our group always rode around the nice parts of town, knowing the cops never wasted their time there. The dubstep was pounding away as we enjoyed it. We carried on and made party plans at Deedee's house for her 21st birthday.

After 15 minutes of driving through the more polished parts of the city, we decided to head to Newark and check out Deedee's new townhouse. Just for the purpose of being excessive, we smoked another joint Deedee had forgotten about in her pocket during the ride. Kathy sped through the entrance and uncomfortably over two giant speed bumps. We all laughed despite being a little startled. Parking made us realize how high we were. We stumbled out instantly, and I dropped my cap-less Pepsi on the ground spilling it all over the place. I picked up the bottle to throw away inside nonchalantly.

As we walked through the door to her house, we were hit with the familiar scent of the sour diesel we loved. Angie walked out of the kitchen and more hugs were exchanged.

"How do you both like the new place?" I asked. It was spacious, and I was pleased to see a balcony connected to the kitchen. Balconies became a necessity for us as smokers, especially those of us who refused to smoke in our homes.

"It's great, and it should be perfect for the wild parties we're going to throw here." Angie happily answered.

Before we got to the house, Angie had already ordered pizza. We turned on some music and discussed our party plans. Bringing a group of white straight men into a party full of gay and bisexual women was a thought that made us crack up. It gave me a rush to consider messing with a few straight white frat boys' egos and influencing the game in my favor. By being the most or one of the most feminine girls there that night, I could easily grab my pick of the litter, Anthony.

It was getting late, judging by the dimming colors outside, so I requested Kathy drop me back off at the dorms. Although I was in for some fun, I felt too exhausted to head to the conventional bars and clubs. I was much more of a smoker than a drinker. Hookah, cigars, cigarettes, and weed were all a part of my beloved college vices. Of course, that list does not include sex, the holy grail of highs.

"Since plans are set in stone now, I will call the rest of the ladies and gents," I said, smiling while deviously raising an eyebrow. Kathy and I headed towards the door to head back to DWU.

"That's cool, Arie. Let us know. See you, Kathy!" Deedee replied to us excitedly as we parted ways. We all knew our last two years of college would be the best. Now that everyone was turning 21, we could legally throw parties! I relished in the idea. The ride home was as fun as usual.

We lit up cigarettes and put the music on the highest possible volume – "Back Again" by Mike Stud featuring Huey Mack played. Kathy loved to speed and drove aggressively. The ride was insane, and while swerving down the road, we rapped to the lyrics in our pathetically feminine pitches. I nervously avoided looking out the front window. We were reckless and often too lucky to learn from our mistakes. She screeched up to the entrance of the upperclassmen dorms. I hopped out, gave her a peace sign, and made my way inside my building. I took the stairs typically because I never had the patience for the elevator.

I opened the door to my room and was surrounded by the soft scent of my lavender diffuser. I sat down at my standard desk and decided to boot up my computer. It was my prized possession after I earned it myself for receiving an academic-based scholarship through the pageant I won. I checked my email inbox, which was empty. My computer was a necessity as I used it to book appearances. Many people don't realize that pageant queens are responsible for their own volunteer work and PR. Outside of my rowdy personal life at college, my year as Miss Delaware was spent prepping, volunteering, and making appearances. After an hour I finished my homework. Another half an hour passed, and I hesitantly booked a couple of appearances. Both the Dover Book Festival and Wilmington Fashion Festival wanted me to attend their events. This seemed easy enough, but I was nervous about how I would style myself.

I decided a cigarette break was earned. The alarm clock on my dresser showed the time was already 8:00 pm. "Damn it," I thought. "Most young men are already getting their plans together now. I better check Facebook." Stubbornly, I refused to opt for a smartphone until I absolutely had to have one for work in 2013. I forced myself away from the tempting app-ridden screen that kept most people distracted from society. Instead, I preferred to live in the physical world.

It felt like forever since I looked at my Facebook, so I opened the personal messages first. There was a long chain message from my close-knit Italian extended family and my mom. Below that was a message from a surgeon who I met two years prior when he was in his last year of medical school. Somewhat annoyed, I opened the DM. His name was Martin, and we met through mutual friends when I was a freshman at DWU. However, after a disappointing birthday where mid date, he left me to go see another woman, I ghosted him for two years.

Martin: Congratulations on your recent accomplishments, beautiful.

Me: …Thanks. How have you been? You know, I liked you a lot and you just ditched me.

Martin: I'm sorry ☹ … Please forgive me, I'd love to see you again. It was a mistake on my part.

Me: Well maybe we can discuss what happened in person.

Martin: Are you free tonight?

Me: Yeah, I just finished my homework.

Martin: Come over – 492 Grass Hill Ct., New Castle, DE

Me: Give me half an hour.

Martin: Ok, let me know when you get here.

CHAPTER 2

Disappointments and Pick-Me-Ups

I stood staring at my computer in shock. "Why did he come back? Did it not work out with his trashy ex-fling? Why do men try to come back when you exile them?" I thought to myself. Without hesitation, I ran to my mirror. My makeup looked lovely, simple but intact despite a day full of smoking. When I wasn't being a beauty queen, I dressed more casually. I had on dark skinny jeans, and a hot pink tank top with black and hot pink Ed Hardy sneakers. My black hair was flat ironed straight with a leopard print bow. It perfectly framed my gold hoop earrings and small, feminine face.

After deciding I looked fine, I threw my purse over my shoulder. Before I left, I grabbed my contact case and birth control pills. I knew this was probably going to be an overnight visit I would regret later. I should have never been so careless with those who already hurt me once before. The only smart decision I made after that was to go without drinking alcohol first.

Driving down to New Castle wasn't a far trip from campus. I played some relaxing hip-hop and enjoyed some new music by my favorite rapper. As I got closer to his house, I noticed I was near one of the nicest town centers in Delaware. "Wow," I thought. "This is a very nice part of town, I guess I'm glad he's doing well." I parked and slyly put out the cigarette I was smoking. I also sprayed a ton of perfume on myself. Lastly, I whipped out my phone, texted him, and waited patiently. After a few minutes, I saw his masculine body walking towards the car. He was a dark-haired, blue-eyed stud who stood about 5'10. He appeared taller with his sexy, toned physique.

I scattered to jump out of my car. Within seconds, we were kissing on each other. Martin knew he had hurt me. Although I never was one to catch feelings on a one-night stand, he was different and intellectually impressive being a surgeon. Two years ago, he was my birthday date after we hung out at a few parties. We tightly hugged then let go to slowly increase the distance that stood between us. Without hesitation, we started to kiss again. I laughed and he turned around, got in front of me, and implied with mannerisms that I mount.

He walked me inside his building piggy-back style. The entire time I was on his back, I whispered to him. "You know I've missed you so much. You just wait until we get in your room." I purred.

Shaking his head in amusement he rang, "It doesn't take a surgeon to figure out your motives, sweetheart. I also have dinner and wine inside."

"I will not be drinking, as you know I have to drive back," I said, in a serious tone.

He set me down outside his door, disapprovingly shook his head at me, and gave me an innocent look. Damn, he was so good at the wolf-in sheep's clothing thing. We went into his condo and violated every room that night. After three hours of rough fornication, we were spent. We attempted to eat the delicately assembled dinner he made but were too exhausted. Our night ended up with us smoking cigarettes and sitting on his balcony together admiring the view of the Wilmington skyline.

"Martin, you know why I came tonight. I want more than this. I want you in my life again." I sighed with relief getting the thought out. I did not want to get hurt but thought it best to put my intentions out in the open. I wouldn't realize until later that this method only worked with genuine people. "We both know that we're young catches in this city. Why don't we pair up for the sake of the events, appearances…and fun? We'd be the most accomplished young couple this city has seen!" I was so enthusiastic and naive. The moment felt right, but I should have known better.

Martin smiled coolly. He paused for a moment, searching for the right words. "Sweetheart, I like your thinking. We can figure things out. Let's take it slow." He was being political. We spent the remaining five minutes discussing our summers. We walked back inside, got back into bed, and cuddled to sleep.

I woke up late the next morning with Martin by my side. It was 10:30 am. "Crap." I thought to myself. "I really ought to get back and make sure all my work is done." I rubbed my love interest's back to wake him up and planted a delicate kiss on his forehead. I said gently, "Hon, I need to head back to school. Want to get dressed and walk me out?"

"Aw, yeah baby. Wish you could stay longer." His voice was like heavenly music to my ears. We both got dressed and I grabbed my things. We walked out and down to my car holding hands. The drive back to campus was slow, and it was drizzling outside. The overcast clouds brought a melancholy mood over the city. It just hit me that I had gone over 12 hours without smoking weed. "Oh yeah, that is exactly what I want right now." I thought. At a stoplight, I put a bit of my stash into a grinder and packed a small amount into my glass pipe. I preferred smoking blunts wrapped with cigarillos, but pipes worked too.

The smoke was harsh and caused me to cough loudly. I finished the pipe with a nice high. Arriving back at my school at about 11:30 am, I made the smart decision to grab lunch. I looked like a hot mess wearing the same outfit I wore out the day before. My makeup was smudged, but I could not have cared less.

I grabbed a bowl instead of a tray and proceeded to eat some cereal. My friend, Leslie, approached. She was a spunky and curvy petite blonde. She usually had a smile on her face and if she didn't, she always had a certain warmth radiating from her. We discussed the weekend, her academic anxiety, and my feelings about Martin. I was convicted of the false belief that we would make a perfect power couple.

At that time, I was too immature to realize the level of my delusional thinking. However, I reveled in the thought of being young and popular. Leslie was my grounded friend who like Frank Sinatra to the mafia, was affiliated with our group, but at the same time unaffiliated. As a pharmacy major, she was normally studying and usually didn't have time for the nonsense. After lunch, I returned to my dorm and finished my homework. I also decided to write flashcards in case one of our professors surprised us with a pop quiz.

It was common for professors at DWU to shock students with pop quizzes. Unlike most colleges, DWU took pride in its unusually low retention rate. The university abided by the basic principle of Darwinian sorts, that the strongest would survive. This meant longer hours studying for more intense exams and learning technology that was beyond the average undergraduate student. Due to the high stress of the environment, and my objection to most beloved study aid drugs, I smoked often. Although I would never recommend someone to take my path, smoking kept me focused.

The week passed at a dragging pace. I began every morning with breakfast, note reviews, and a blunt. With senior year approaching, I knew I had a limited time to party like a twenty-year-old. On Wednesday of that week, I made a bet with Kathy that I could smoke 7 blunts at Deedee's party on my own, in a row. She bet me back that she could smoke 11 blunts. Whoever failed was to buy pizza and if we both lost, we'd split it. However, if we both won, we determined the reward would be a "special" brownie party. Thursday came fast and I texted Anthony to alert him of the plans and to coordinate carpooling.

Me: Hey there! :*

Anthony: What's the deal?

Me: We're celebrating tomorrow, think you can ring up your attractive bros?

Anthony: Fuck yeah, I already have three friends who want to experience a DWU party.

Me: Haha, awesome, I'm so glad I hit you up. Let

me know what time you want me to pick you up. Party starts at 10 pm and is in Newark.

Anthony: Oh cool, that's not far. You can head over our way around 10:00!

Me: Sounds good, Jenny and I will be there.

I looked up from my phone and mouthed "yes!" I knew I was going to have sex and at that point, it had been about a week. It always made me angry to be told women could get laid whenever they wanted. That is the worst hook-up related bullshit women are told. No, we as women cannot control who is attracted to and who is repulsed by us. I fucking wished.

I finished my homework and decided to take a blunt ride. I sat at my desk and used my grinder to break up the top-shelf bud I recently picked up. A half-ounce of medical grade marijuana sat in front of me. It was more than I ever had in my personal possession before. A quarter of it was to be used for my seven blunts and the rest was for unplanned recreational use. I meticulously dispersed the green plant within the tobacco paper and licked it to seal it neatly.

During the walk to my car, I reflected on how fortunate I was. I felt like a real queen and quite honestly, a bad bitch. I was the master of my fate, and I was ready to take everything I wanted, including sex. Grabbing my keys, I attempted to have some style while unlocking my car despite the lack of an audience. It was important to me to appear cool, calm, and collected. Perhaps it's because these aspects of my personality were the same ones that I was the most insecure about. The ride was short but soothing. I parked my car in the commuter lot knowing that I did not have to move my car until the next morning.

My night's sleep went by peacefully and I awoke to smoke another bit of Mary Jane. The car ride around the wealthy neighboring community made me feel apathetic. I didn't care what consequences I could face for my actions. Act first, apologize later were the words I lived by religiously. I woke up late, so I skipped breakfast and rolled into class wearing fluffy pink fleece sweatpants with a navy zip-up. I looked like Ohio threw up on me. Friday classes took forever as usual with a pace that seemed competitive to a snail. At lunch I texted Kathy.

Me: What it do tho?!
Kathy: Party, right?
Me: Truth. LOL

Our conversation was purposeless aside from validating my boredom. I was finally in my last class of the day. Jesus Christ, does this crap ever get faster?

THE DAY ENDED!!!! YAY!!!! With all my energy I rushed from the classroom to my dorm. I showered quickly and put my hair in rollers. I swapped the clothes I was wearing for something more party appropriate. I chose dark short shorts, tight black knee-high boots, and a solid black Ed Hardy tank top. There always had to be something in my hair to indicate my femininity whether it was a bow or flower. My choice that night was a bright red rose. Having a girly hair accessory made me feel comfortable with my sometimes stylistically mismatched attire.

The time was already 6 pm and since I finished getting ready, I thought it would be a smart idea to eat dinner. Although I was always averse to drinking, I knew that night peer pressure would get to me anyway. My choices were greasy food or a salad. I chose the salad with a side of bread, assuming the combination would help make my likely alcohol consumption easier.

At 8 pm, I decided to head out to Jenny's house which was out of the way in Talleyville. Being diligent I packed away my stash so I could pace my intake throughout the night. I hadn't forgotten the bet Kathy and I wagered, and I certainly was not the type who backed down from a challenge. The drive up was beautiful as the descending sun made its way down to sleep. The moon was rising, clearly ready to party with us. Everything felt as magical as it could be.

My car pulled into Jenny's driveway at about 8 pm. Before my car was in park, I saw a petite figure running towards me. I got out, squeezed Jenny, and spun her around like a little sister.

"MY BOO!!!" I sang out.

"Arie! God damn this summer was too long. It felt like it had been years." She replied in the same uplifted tone. "So, what's up with this party? I know Deedee's throwing it, what's the occasion?"

"GIRL! It's our sister's 21st, the big '2' '1', the heaven of age!" I said in an announcer tone.

"Oh yeah! That's awesome, come up with me while I change out of this. We should hit up a liquor store to pick her up some birthday bottles."

Jenny was the first to turn 21 with a late summer birthday and didn't mind hitting up the store for us. She was a sensitive person who dealt with a tragic young adulthood. She would not be able to drive again until she went a year without a seizure. We would count the months together. One time she went 10 months only to go into an episode 7 weeks before being cleared. We weren't in a perfect world all the time, but we leaned on one another.

While following her up to her room, I was playfully nudged at by her two American Pit Bulls. Jenny began hollering and they immediately transformed into two scared Chihuahuas sent away by their mama. It took another hour before she was fully ready. She decided on a blue sequence tank top, white shorts, and heels. We both looked the other over to ensure nothing looked weird or was out of place.

By the time we made it to the liquor store, we were late to pick up the boys. We didn't want to be disrespectful to Deedee and show up empty-handed, so Jenny ran into the store. I received a text while waiting.

Anthony: Arie, where the hell are you?

Me: I grabbed Jenny up in Talleyville, it was out of the way! Now we're getting booze. We'll literally be at DMU in ten.

Anthony: Alright, alright. Chill, you know I love giving you a tough time.

Me: Of course, you do. My discomfort is your comedy.

Anthony: I promise, tonight you won't feel any discomfort.

Anthony: Quit being a brat and come pick us up.

Jenny opening the door startled me immediately. She laughed in response, realizing she completely caught me off guard. My phone screen was still lit, and she looked down. She read the messages and jokingly shook her head at me.

"You know I'm a horn dog, don't act shocked. Glad to see you got the booze, let's go." I declared.

We sped through a few neighborhoods until we arrived at the DMU dorms. I texted Anthony who confirmed he was on his way down with his friends. Jenny and I decided to smoke a cigarette together while we waited. All the sudden my car was practically bum rushed by recognizable frat boys shaking the frame. I yelled out the window and the boys stopped. I then got out of the car and embraced my college crush.

"Well, hellooo Miss Delaware. Great to see you. Let's head to that party." He looked at me differently than in the past when we had hung out. He was ready to play with a newly single snack. God damn it, Anthony always knew how to turn me on and I hated it so much. He brought four of his friends, Matt (his roommate), Jake, Andy, and Kristian. We all looked at Jenny and I gestured for her to scoot or sit on a lap. Somehow, we successfully crammed five bulky men and us ladies into my car. The ride to Newark was a little uncomfortable, but comedic. I blasted the appropriate playlist of dubstep music while terrifying the boys with my reckless driving.

When we arrived, it was already 11 pm and the party was banging. We parked in a close spot and scattered out of the car. The guys were all thrilled and conveniently single. I walked through the door first with the boys and Jenny behind me.

21

"Oh and look who the fuck decided to show up. And you brought guests too!" Kathy laughed and hugged me.

"Yeah, this is Anthony, he's a friend of mine from DMU." I cheerfully replied.

"Nice to meet you, Kathy, these are my friends Matt, Jake, Andy, and Kristian. Anyway, where's the birthday girl?!" Anthony interjected.

"She's in the kitchen, you guys want some shots?" Jenny questioned trying to be polite.

"Hell yeah, buddy! Let's get these boys drunk." I stated.

The gents walked through the doors to the kitchen. Kathy pulled me back.

"Ready to get this bet on?" She asked.

"Oh, you know I am. I doubt I can out smoke you, but I know I can smoke 7 blunts."

I proceeded to make my way into the kitchen and began to roll my first blunt of the night. I pulled out half my stash since I had it split between two bags. One was for me and the rest for the party and after. Unexpectedly, Anthony eased his way behind me and wrapped his arms around me. I savored the moment. If I had to choose between Anthony and Martin, Anthony would win based on sex and looks alone.

"What ya' doin' Arie? Don't you want a drink?" he whispered into my ear.

"Dear I have an especially important bet to win. I can't be distracted with drinking this second but enjoy yourself." I retorted.

"What kind of bet?"

"I have to smoke 7 blunts alone before the end of the night."

"Well, that's a little greedy." He sounded disappointed. To his surprise, I pulled out my other bag and waved it in front of his face.

"That's why I brought some for the party too. Here, I'll roll two. One to pass and one for me."

I rolled them right in time as Deedee and Angie were announcing a round of beer pong.

Anthony and I walked out to the balcony as people came inside. His friends were already in the living room beginning the game and it hit me that this was the first time we were alone. I waited to make a move and instead lit my blunt. I gave him the group blunt and we smoked together. To my relief and severe sexual tension, Jenny popped her head out.

"I heard coughing! Ya'll smoking without me?" Jenny innocently inquired.

"On the contrary it's nice to have you out here. Let's smoke!!!" I ceremoniously replied. The three of us chatted, coughed, and joked. I figured I was still sober enough that I could efficiently smoke another, so I rolled another and did. At this point, I was beginning to feel a little buzzed. Wisely I chose to run back inside for a round of waters and drinks for Jenny and Anthony.

While walking in I bumped into Jake, Anthony's friend from their college's baseball team. He was a little taller and lankier than Anthony. However, he was a blonde-haired blue-eyed piece of prime ass. He handed me the same test tube shot from the group I saw Deedee pouring some suspect liquid in earlier, so I gladly took it. To my disappointment, it ended up being rum, ewww. We looked at each other for a couple seconds until I shook my head and walked off. "I don't have time for all these bitches. Focus Arie." I thought to myself.

I walked out with the drinks and noticed a few more party goers joined Anthony and Jenny on the balcony. I handed them their drinks and sipped on my water. I only had five more to go. "How hard could this be?" I said to myself.

While smoking my fourth blunt it hit me how terribly fucked up I was, despite only having one shot. This was a different high than I was used to. This was a deep seated, brain cell killing and throat cancer-causing high. Anthony and Jenny only were on #2 split between 4-5 people. Kathy stumbled out onto the balcony.

"I'm at...I think I'm at 6." Kathy said clearly feeling the weight of this challenge.

"I'm on 4 but it's only midnight. As long as I can get one in an hour for the rest of the party, I'll be set. I feel it, bro." I said noticing her spaced out look.

I walked back inside to check what was going on. Crystal and Kendra were entertaining with a free style rap. The party was still wild, people around were doing whippits, playing kings and beer pong taking up most of the floor space. I realized I hadn't used the bathroom since I left school, so I ran upstairs. The room was nicely decorated and had a typical but pretty beach theme. An awkward knock from the door sounded.

"Someone's in here!" I yelled in a strong, feminine tone.

"I know. Let me in Arie." I knew that the familiar voice was Anthony. I was a little shocked he followed me upstairs. At the same time, I was relieved he made the move, even if it was a little bizarre. At 20 years old,

I lived for the game of hooking up but was shy with execution. Without saying anything, I pulled up my shorts, washed my hands, flushed the toilet, opened the door, and pulled him in.

While we were making out, he locked the door behind him. My senses went berserk, and I could feel myself getting aroused. Forcefully, he undid the button on my shorts and then he unzipped them. At the same time, I was pulling his pants down. He felt up my thighs between my legs and I gasped. It was euphoric to feel him playing with me. After some foreplay, he spun me around and bent me over the sink. I felt his throbbing dick penetrate me as he moaned loudly. It was impossible to be quiet with how amazing it was and I knew Deedee would be fine with my escapade. I looked up at the mirror and watched him fuck me. He was so dreamy, even though the clear mirror view was completely obliterated by a storm of booze and drugs.

He had a distinguished look with an appealing handsome face and my favorite shade of blue eyes. Beads of sweat started to form on his forehead and across his sharp black hairline. My immature and plastered brain just kept thinking about how good I felt and how pretty I thought he was.

We lasted a good twenty minutes before we both finished. Someone knocked on the door and we decided to stop hogging the room. With no poise or grace, I tripped out and Anthony laughed at me as he stabilized me with his arm. The line of three people did not look amused. We sheepishly made our way downstairs holding hands. As we walked down, I saw the most awkward faux pas between Matt, Deedee, and Angie. Matt had never met lesbians and was asking some questions which sounded offensive. The two were used to this so it didn't faze them. As I overheard them responding in upbeat voices, my worry faded.

The next three blunts were going to suck, but a bet is a bet. Plus, I hated losing. I joined Kathy and rolled more blunts both for the group and myself. I was able to stomach two more, but my throat was aching. Kathy was on ten and I was on six. This was just excessive, but my 20-year-old brain was too high to care.

Kathy and I hugged as we lit our last two blunts. Meanwhile, the group on the balcony turned into a crowd. Word got around the party that we were breaking party toking records. They began cheering us on as we toked and coughed. It was finally done. Thank God. I don't think I would have been able to drive home that night had I smoked more. Afterward, I decided to head back inside and sip on some Pepsi to get caffeine in me. The crisp cold taste of the soda eased my throat pain.

By the time Kathy and I finished our bet, we were both voiceless and miserable. The party eventually began to die down. I sat outside with Kathy and had a heart to heart with her while the boys passed out around the house. Her hair glowed under the moonlight but I had a sense of sadness we couldn't be together. Pageantry wouldn't allow it. She was my closest friend and the most beautiful person I knew. Much later, I searched the room and Jenny was on the couch passed out with Crystal.

I gently tugged Jenny's arm. "Wake up!" I hissed. I looked at my phone and it was already 4:30 am.

"Oh shit. We're done partying already? That's cool, I'm done. Can I sleep at your place?" Jenny tiredly asked while getting up.

"Yeah hon, that's why I bought out my room this year. More room for guests!"

Jenny and I grabbed our stuff but could not find the guys. We were annoyed that we may have gotten ditched. In the dark, warm early fall evening we headed to my car. As we drove down to the community gate, we saw a cluster of young men. It was the boys looking for a taxi as if they were in downtown Wilmington. This site was phenomenally hilarious, but Jenny and I were able to convince them to hop in for a ride home. While whizzing through the empty streets, everyone was yawning. We were ten minutes from our schools when the boys demanded we stop for Wendy's. Since Anthony put out and was well behaved at the party, I complied.

The drive-thru cashier sounded exasperated to take our order. It did not help that no one knew what they wanted and were sloppily yelling orders at the poor girl. Finally, she got our order and we drove to the window. Up until this point, I had a perfect night and that's exactly when Murphy's Law came to visit. That moment Anthony projectile vomited out the window down the side of my car.

"Really?!" I yelled. "I am coming back to your school tomorrow, and you are cleaning this shit up." The guys looked at me frightened as if I seemed like I was going to kick them out. Instead, I shook my head and encouraged everyone to drink and eat up. My nurturing motherly instincts were stronger than my angry fatherly ones.

We finally got to DMU and I got out of the car to hug Anthony. Within seconds he was gone, beckoning his bros back to their apartments. I was stunned. My head dropped and I got into my car. Jenny passed out again and instead of waking her, I left her undisturbed until we arrived on campus.

"Hey sweetie, let's head up, we're here," I said softly and nudged her.

"Oh, my lord… tonight was insane." She replied.

"I agree and I loved every second of it." I grinned satisfied with the night, despite the vomit dripping down my front passenger door.

My previous weekend of partying was a whirlwind, but it was the third week of school and the first month of my reign as Miss Delaware. The reality hit me hard. I was suffering from a hardcore case of the Mondays. The week dragged on and I studied substantially for my first round of exams. I tried to look at my Dover Book Festival appearance as the light at the end of the tunnel. Throughout the week, I flirted heavily with Anthony and Martin via text. I didn't necessarily want a relationship, but I desired a confidant and protective spotlight partner to escort me during appearances.

What seemed like a dream became a nightmare by Friday. I was returning to campus from my after class blunt ride with Kathy when Martin began texting me.

Martin: Hey sweetheart. We need to talk.

Me: What's up handsome? Having a rough night on call?

Martin: Sort of…. Hey look we need to stop talking for a few months.

Me: WHAT?! WTH? Why?

Martin: It's complicated to explain but we can talk again in a few months. I just need to sort out some issues.

I hesitated to respond while walking indignantly into my building. I was livid at his obviously bullshit excuse and was not amused at all. When returning to my room I texted him again.

Me: I guess at this point, I only have questions to ask…. Why even bother? What is so appealing about me that you'd even "want to come back"?

Martin: You're adorable.

"That's IT?! THAT FUCKING ASSHOLE!" I roared furiously and slammed my phone on the desk. "That's it. I'm done with this clown. Done. No third chance, no fourth. None of that." I felt my ex's, and Martin's behavior validated my promiscuity. How could I trust one of these horrible monsters more amicably known as men?

I decided to text Anthony and forget about Martin. After a short conversation, he invited me over to smoke. I happily obliged and spent the night. We smoked, hooked up twice, and cuddled. His solid masculine body fit perfectly as the big spoon to my little spoon. The following morning, I woke up fast aware of my appearance later that day. I kissed Anthony goodbye and told him I looked forward to our next hook up sesh.

When I got back on campus, I darted to my room

and rushed to get ready for my first appearance as a beauty queen. I took a five-minute break and looked outside. The campus was naturally beautiful with birds bathing in the fountains and squirrels frolicking on the freshly cut dewy grass. It seemed more serene than an environment I could ever deserve. I turned around and faced my bright pink dorm room. The concept of forgetting anything gave me real anxiety. Noticing my hands were shaking, I made the decision to smoke a cigarette on the way. Keys in one hand, crown box and purse in the other, I walked down to my car.

After I found my destination, I parked in a parking garage to avoid being seen before the event. I smoked the cigarette in my hand as fast as possible. Using perfume, hand sanitizer, and hair spray I was able to cover my repulsive smoked out scent. Checking the mirror with satisfaction, I threw my purse into my glove box. I then changed into a dress I had in a bag without taking my clothes off. While riding the elevator down, I put on my pageant regalia. I straightened the banner as the door opened.

Exiting the parking garage, I was overwhelmed by the attention almost immediately. As I walked down the sidewalk to the festival, people kept reading my banner calling me by my title.

"Miss Delaware! Where are you from?!" a woman cheered on the opposite side of the road.

"Thank you so much, I'm from Wilmington! Enjoy the book festival!" I smiled, feeling well received by the audience of strangers. When I arrived at the volunteer tent, I was warmly greeted by the host, Delaware Promotion and Arts. They determined I would be most useful reading to the kids at story time and walking around mingling. The job was an enjoyable success, and my day went off without a hitch. Several little girls wanted my autograph and to try on my crown. Appearing was a fascinating way to interact with the public and something I grew used to very quickly. It made me feel energized and socially intelligent. In the back of my mind, I knew these moments would be fleeting so I didn't complain about the extra time it took from my schedule.

CHAPTER 3

Heroic Failure

A month passed and October was welcome to us freaks who liked using it as excuse to dress slutty. The morning air was getting cooler, and the leaves were already changing to their vibrant rainbow of fall hues. I wish I could say Anthony and I ended up together. He instead chose to pursue a British chick from his frat's sister sorority. Although DMU was originally an all-men's college in the early 90s, they changed their rules to accommodate women. While I respected Anthony's choice, I could not help but be bitter. In a way, it felt like a small failure on my behalf. After three disappointing attempts at trying to be in a relationship, I decided to put it all on hold temporarily.

Midterms began and the air in every classroom was tense with mutual disdain and stress. Weed helped my test anxiety and made it possible for me to calmly take exams. Each one was a different demon which I needed to defeat. Studying up to four hours a day drastically increased my pot consumption. Sadly, my coffee consumption increased simultaneously. My teeth began to get some stains, so I got some white strips, which took care of my "midterm marks."

While taking midterms I avoided contact with any

men. When I received my grades by the end of the week, I went right back to celebrating. This was another wonderful excuse to have more sex and get ripped. Kathy and I took a blunt ride around town and discussed how a month prior we both won the bet - WHICH MEANT MAGIC BROWNIES. She dropped me back off at my dorm with a plan to bake them and hang out the next week.

I decided to run errands and I headed to CVS. On my drive, I noticed the fiery red and sunshine colors of the falling leaves. Things were changing both seasonally and metaphorically in my life. For the first time, I felt liberated. The trip was a short one and only took ten minutes. I hated shopping and being decisive was a personal value of mine. I parked, ran in, grabbed the products I wanted, and just as fast, paid and got back in my car. On the slow ride back, I wondered what else was going to change. I was in my fourth year of competing in pageantry and was warned that everything shifts with a state title. We must carefully monitor our online appearance and act "ladylike" or risk losing our jobs. We "couldn't" be seen at bars, clubs or parties.

Pulling onto campus, I noticed the incredible lack of activity. Since it was a Friday, it made complete sense that everyone went home. Aside from the occasional parties my group threw, the school was usually dead. I turned to head to the upperclassmen dorms. Turning the corner, I sped up as I usually did for fun. However, my view of grandeur changed to a view of horror. A student was pushing her SUV up a hill. She was clearly struggling and looked to be in distress. My instincts took over and I slammed my brakes. Since the campus was empty, I had no issue parking my car in place on the drive.

With all the speed I could conjure, I unlatched my seat belt, opened the door, and darted for the woman. Time seemed to slow down at that moment. The leaves fell gracefully as the autumn colors became a blur. It wasn't until I watched her body get pummeled, that I realized time sped up, and I was too late. Thinking on my feet, I chased her car down the hill to the neighboring university. When the massive vehicle smashed against their campus fence, I was relieved that it did not hurt anyone else. I opened the car door and reached in the center console for the poor stranger's purse and phone. It was exactly where I was hoping it would be. After retrieving her purse, I ran back up the hill with it, only to find her lying motionless on the ground. The coat I had on was my favorite, but this was a more worthy cause. I slowly lifted her head carefully so as not to hurt her more and moved my coat underneath her neck.

Soon, a crowd began to form which made me livid. "Can't you see this woman is in trauma?! Stop crowding her, give her air and do something instead of standing around like an audience!" I screamed at other DWU students. Some stayed to watch but others did obey my orders. I called 911 as Leslie came down from the dorms with a bottle of water and towel. The ambulance and police arrived soon after. I gave them her purse and phone to identify her but I felt lost.

The responders thanked me for helping and promised me an update as soon as possible. This became one of the most memorable days of my life in community service. There had to be more I could do and other people I could actually help. The guilt from failing to save this woman hit me like a brick. Despite what any therapist could tell me, it felt like my fault she was unconscious laying in front of me. I was relieved to find out a few days later, she had a sprained ankle, but no broken bones or head damage. Other than recovering from that and a couple of wounds she was going to be ok.

As they took her (and my favorite coat), I made my way back up to the dorms. I was happy to give up my coat for this incident, but my ego was crushed and I felt defeated by fate. One of my DWU acquaintances ran up to me inappropriately smirking. I was confused as I listened to her tone and watched her body language.

"Were you the one who saw the woman get run over?! That's so funny and crazy!" She said with little thought on the situation.

"It wasn't fucking funny and yes I found her while others stood around watching." I responded harshly, "Stupid bitch." Then I walked down the hall and slammed the door to my room.

My next hour was spent pacing and overthinking. Was she going to be ok? How do you merely get over watching someone getting run over by a car? How could this even happen at DWU? Why didn't the universe let me get run over instead? Nothing about that day made sense to me. I wondered about how and when I was going to find out if she was okay. Realizing that my stress did me little good in the moment, I decided to fall back on my comforts of smoking and sexing. I immediately messaged Anthony.

Me: OMG. I just had the worst day ever.

Anthony: What happened!?

Me: So basically, I tried to save a woman before she got run over by her car. She didn't have the e-brake on and the car was facing downhill. I tried to save her but I failed.

Anthony: Oh shit.....Well I'm with my girl right now but you can come over. We're probably going to pass out soon, but Matt and the guys are here. I'm sure they wouldn't mind keeping you some company while you process things.

Me: Thanks hon, I'll be over within the hour.

I looked around my room to make sure I had everything. My mind was not in the place to care whether I looked good or not. The event kept replaying in my head. Before leaving I rolled a couple of blunts to bring with me to help ease the pain. It was an emotionally troubling task to stifle my crying. As I walked to my car, cool teardrops ran down my cheeks. "Why does nothing make sense right now? It was best to not cry," I thought, as I convinced myself to stop tearing up.

I drove to the DMU apartments and made my way up to the guys' room. My hand hardly reached the door and it swung back in the opposite direction. Anthony was waiting and gave me a huge hug. He apologized that he could not hang out, but he wanted to at least make sure I was alright before he rejoined his girlfriend. I told him I was okay, and it was healthy for me to be in a place with friends where I felt comfortable. With my reassurance, he said goodnight and retreated to his bedroom. Matt followed his behavior and gave me a huge hug. He was extra gentlemanly and proceeded to hang up my jacket in his closet.

Kristian, Jake, and Andy sat in the living room anxiously waiting to hear my story about the chaos. I began speaking, and I pulled out the blunts. "We can pass both, I think we'll need it tonight." I sniffed trying not to cry again.

"Hey, it's fine, you've clearly been through hell." Kristian innocently replied. They could tell I was disheveled and not my normal self. I adjusted my hair after taking a few hits. As if they could read my mind, Matt looked at Jake and Kristian, then back at me.

"Arie no worries, you're still hot as fuck," Matt said in a straightforward tone. This made me lose it, giggle hysterically and broke me out of my dark cloud. Either that or something else needed to be said for comedic relief. I calmly reported the account of my failure. They tried reassuring me that it was not my fault. Unfortunately, their message was ineffective, and I decided to digress from the original conversation topic. Instead, we discussed the upcoming Halloween party Andy's frat was throwing. The first blunt was done and the mood softened in the room. Matt brought out some wine which made me even calmer. It wasn't my choice drink for parties, but it was a great option for a relaxing night in.

As we smoked and drank more, the mood started to change hues. My demeanor was strongly enhanced by being phenomenally drunk and high. The couch was a large L shape, so we could all comfortably sit on it together. I laid down my head and crossed my arms beneath it on Matt's crotch. Surprisingly, Andy started feeling up my legs and Jake began stroking my back. I stretched out a bit to enjoy the rush of sensation I was feeling throughout my body. That's right…I'm still a badass queen. Kristian took my wine glass for me and gave me a questioning facial expression. I smiled back wickedly and nodded in approval. This was truly my favorite coping mechanism. Having fun in the bedroom and transcending conventional behavior as a woman made me feel invincible.

Two years prior, I experienced my first and only orgy up to that point. Including myself it was two men and women which was well-balanced. However, I always wanted to dabble in the unknown territory of one woman/multiple men orgies, improperly named gang bangs. I slinked out of their hands, got up, and wagged my butt like a tail in front of their thirsty gazes.

"Come and get it." I teased as I shook my backside at them. This prompted Matt to get up, throw me over his shoulder and carry me into his bedroom. He dropped me on the bed dominantly. The guys followed and Kristian grabbed a bottle of gin. Matt dimmed the lights and turned on the music. To my pleasure, it was my favorite sex and workout genre — dubstep.

Their collective touch on my little body was electrifying. I found each of them attractive in their own way. My soul felt completely spoiled but also quite deserving. "I keep my body hot and reputation polished, so I fucking deserve this." I thought to myself. We tried several positions that were audacious. Kristian made me orgasm over and over as the other three took a break and watched. I took turns and rode each of them while using my hands and mouth to pleasure the other sexy men.

The entire affair took a little over two hours. It was the steamiest night I had ever experienced. I did not feel regret after and swiftly returned to my bubbly self. The orgy made me feel worshipped and sexually powerful. Men always talk a big game about MWW threesomes, but it takes a particularly masculine, secure man to do it the other way around. To them, it was like sharing their favorite restaurant or hobby. I was doing exactly what I wanted to, how I wanted to while metaphorically making "feminine expectations" my bitch. I didn't believe real cross-culture feminism was to gain equality. Instead, I thought it was trying to dominate the privileged ones how they've dominated everyone else. My flawed thinking hadn't caught up with me yet, but I was riding a wave of toxic behavior and femininity. I bargained with myself - I was only doing what men have been doing to women since the beginning of time.

Deciding to be even more of a baddie, I rejected a cuddling session afterward. I told them I'd call later. The guys hung around watching me leave. "Yeah," I thought to myself, "Fuck it." I decided thoughtfully that I wouldn't go to the DMU frat party for Halloween. It was a bad plan for the sake of hooking up to constantly accept invitations from the boys. At some points, I had to play hard to get. The deep chill outside reminded me it was fall and that I lost my favorite coat failing to save someone. I returned to my dorm room at 3:30 am and fell drained into bed.

The next morning, I woke up at 10:30 am and like a princess, I laid in my bed for a bit while looking out my Victorian style window. The trees still had most of their leaves but watching them thin made me apathetic to the day. I thanked God for not having class on midterm break. The day and night before were too crazy for me to even begin to process. My final decision on my Halloween plan was to head to my friend Vlad's house. Vlad and his girlfriend Natasha threw the best parties, admittedly better than Deedee.

Vlad came from wealth and was an heir with dual citizenship. Natasha was a brilliant and stunning mathematician studying for multiple certifications while in undergrad. They were proud young Russians who smoked and partied every weekend. Kathy was out of town visiting her current love interest with Deedee. My next move was to coordinate.

Me: Bro!! What's up, are you guys having a
Halloween party next weekend?
Vlad: Yeah man, it's Friday night, come thru!

My body was still a bit shaky from the night before, so I went to the gym to relieve my tension before venturing to the cafeteria for breakfast. Upon completing breakfast, my internal smoking clock went off. Instead of sitting on campus, I decided on a shoreline drive to reflect on my emotions. Hitting the road was relaxing and I loved a random scenic ocean ride. The coast was only an hour from campus and I continued south to my heart's desire. Winter was coming as the houses on the beach had front yards covered in dying leaves.

Alone I reflected on what happened to the woman I watched get run over. There had to be something more I could do for society, and I was determined. It also hit me the upcoming national competition was only a month away. Prepping for pageantry was as much a part of my routine as smoking but was far less easy. My community service and title were coming together to form a bigger picture.

"I must leave this world a better place than it is now." I said out loud to myself. This phrase began a huge turning point in my life. I never felt guilty for indulging or having fun, but I also knew I had to find a balance at some point. Here was an opportune moment for such a transformation to take place. If only it were so linear or simple.

Late fall was almost over but Thanksgiving was one of the most remarkable weeks of my life. The organization I was a state queen for hosted their national competition during the holiday to avoid contestants having conflicts with work or school. My national pageant, Miss America National was the most popular pageant in terms of aspiring contestants. It was hosted annually in LA. Even the org's state competitions saw profit above other prestigious programs. Each state had seven age groups with hefty entry fees. Within the seven age groups, about 50-250 contestants competed in each division.

Prior to Miss America National, I made sure to be "national ready". When winning Miss Delaware, part of my prize was a full coaching and styling package. My coach and her stylist were a fantastic team dedicated to prepping me one to two times every week. My figure looked great, my full wardrobe was organized, and my ducks were in a row. Although packing ended up being the biggest pain, I was privileged to make the trip an adventure with my mother. The flights out of Philadelphia were easy to get through.

The week-long event itself was filled with competitive enthusiasm. Every young lady competing was smart, beautiful and a state winning titleholder. The atmosphere is completely different at any national pageant. At this level, the competition is stronger and more equally deserving. Judges who are appointed for nationals claim their job as one of the hardest there and nobody questions that. I know saying this would lose me points, but it's easy to compete when you love it. It came naturally for me to do every step necessary to be a top contender. There were two types of pageant girls, clappers and contenders. The contenders were the top 5 up front with the crowns, banners and trophies. The clappers were the girls behind them during the finale and nobody wanted to be a clapper.

My new sisters and I got along well enough. They were all sweet girls but difficult to read. Pageant queens usually aren't catty due to image reasons. It's considered highly distasteful to bring any drama to a pageant. The industry is so strict that young ladies who are anything but ecstatic to be there, are permanently marked as having bad sportsmanship within the community. It did not help that bloggers began following pageant queens and remarking on us as contestants. I was known for being a little too anxious on stage but praised for my on-point physique.

To my disappointment, I did not win the overall top score. However, I was in shock when it was revealed I won the modeling portion and was the newly crowned Miss National Model 2011-2012. It was upsetting to lose the big title, but a small blessing to win a preliminary one. My prize included a collegiate scholarship and an invitation to sign with the pageant's sister agency.

CHAPTER 4

A Night to Remember

The snow in December gave me nostalgic feelings about the upcoming holiday. Every year DWU had a snow man building competition, which prompted students to get festive. It prompted my group of friends to build snow boobs and phallic blobs. Dorm windows had Santa and reindeer decals with holiday lights. Many of the ladies' doors had some sort of decoration and it gave the campus a warmer feel. Conversations around the dorms revolved around plans for Christmas break. It was my favorite time of year. To me, it was unbelievable how fast this semester went by.

While my friends kept chatting at lunch about holiday plans, I sat quietly knowing I made an unpopular decision. I wanted to get credits out of the way early so I could have an enjoyable senior year. Instead of making plans, I chose to do an on-campus winter semester during break. However, we all knew finals for the fall were approaching. This made the holiday mood a little less joyous.

Finals seemed to take forever but I was glad to get them over with. Before the winter semester started, I returned to Ohio for a week to see my family for Christmas. I chose to only be social with two friends from my middle and high school days. One of them, Cara attended our rival high school. The other, Trisha was a friend since elementary school.

Returning home did not end up as badly as I expected. I was able to ignore my ex from high school and reunite with my two best friends. It was upsetting but necessary to abstain from communication with my ex-sweetheart. Instead, spending time with my two old friends made for a lovely distraction.

With the lack of activities, I was depressed coming back to my school in January 2012. The grounds resembled a ghost town since most students were still home for the holiday. It was concerning that my schedule was going to get busier and my life more disciplined. Hope and optimism in my future kept me fueled. Somehow, I'd find a way to balance everything. I made the spontaneous decision to start volunteering with my local fire department as a dispatcher and classroom educator. The training was vigorous and information intensive. Being resolute to make a positive mark on society, I passed all the courses.

The only winter course I had with DWU, was Personal Finance. Although the class was not difficult, it was a long, dragged out 6 hours every Saturday. One of my favorite professors in the department was teaching the course, which made the inconvenience somewhat better. He was thorough with lessons but only because his tests were incredibly hard. It was normal for students to study for 8-10 hours just to pass his midterm. During the week I would volunteer two shifts, study and organize spring state queen appearances.

The month went by slowly but I found it productive enough. Being without many of my usual social companions and fuck toys, I became lonely. Two weeks into the semester I decided to do something stupid and create an online dating profile. It was a strange new tool that I never thought to take advantage of. Regrettably, the lack of ass and a significant other was getting to me. Through the website, I met an interesting variety of men. The first was an athletic pre-med student at Delaware State University, who only had sex with one other woman in his life. He disdained confident women but expected his love interest to be successful. Of course, with my personality, that didn't last longer than a week. To be honest the sex with him sucked, so it's not like it damaged my confidence or hook up prospects. With little success, I decided to leave my pursuits in the real world where I knew how to get laid.

Between all my activities, the winter term felt shorter than I assumed it would. My friends were finally moving back into the dorms, unaware that while they were gone, they took the social ambiance with them. The campus wasn't as picturesque without students to fill up the dining hall and hallways. Time was diminishing and I often thought of the time left in my reign as Miss Delaware. The fire department was organizing two huge Wilmington based events and invited me to chair both. Project Prom Night was a project which raised money for house fire victims by collecting gently used prom dresses and selling them. The other event which fell on my 21st birthday was Fiery Night, a grand gala to raise money for and celebrate the fire department.

With time dwindling, I feared that I would be

forced to attend these events alone. I sat in my room on a quiet Sunday morning in February, before spring classes began. My schedule included 6 classes which were mostly finance and technology focused. It was intimidating to think about balancing everything while attempting to date. Matters were made challenging with Anthony's friends as they continued to request more group sex. I wanted to drop everything to mess around with them, but my schedule was burning me out. I decided to call my mom for the first time of the day.

"Hey Arie, how is everything?" my mother happily chirped.

"Mom…I have been so depressed. I just really wish I found someone. To be honest, I even made one of those weird online dating profiles." I said in a broken tone. "Not to mention two important events are coming up with the fire department that I have to appear at as Miss Delaware!!!!"

"Sweetie, try not to worry. You can't rush these sorts of things." My mom sounded like she pitied her baby. "Also, you HAVE to be careful with that stuff. What if some guy comes and abducts you?!" Her tone shifted from sorry for me to worrying. I internally died of humor by her typical response.

"Mom that's the least of my worries. I always meet guys in public. Although I've had no real luck with any of my dates." I said assertively. The conversation ended with her attempted reassurance, which as usual was unsuccessful in the area of romance.

Both my room and soul felt hollow. I pined and longed for someone who could join me on this fun journey. At that point, most of my other state sister queens had boyfriends. I judged myself as stupid and immature to feel so sad over not having a boyfriend. I sat down, looked down at the college provided pale wood desk and opened one of the drawers. It was pathetic that weed was the only thing that could lift my mood. The batch of weed was particularly purple. The THC crystals sparkled in front of my eyes.

The third drawer down contained my stash box and cigarillos that I rolled blunts with. The green was easy to grind and filled the split rillo nicely. With a final lick and look-over, I slid it into my small brown Coach bag. Majestic flurries of snow surrounded campus buildings and a strong breeze swept by as I made my way to my car. I almost lost my footing and slipped on the winter-slick road. Opening my car door posed another challenge as it was frozen shut.

"Fuck!" I ruefully yelled to no one. With way too strong of a pull, I was able to open the door and fall on my ass. "Fucking Christ!" I said and then under my breath said, "ok sorry God, I know that wasn't your fault." I tried to get up a couple times until I finally pushed myself back up, brushing the snow off. Before getting into my car, I looked around humiliated but was relieved to see no one. The music filled the car when I turned the key. I took the blunt out of my purse and drove off.

Driving through the wealthy neighborhood parallel to the school was a default choice. My head nodded back and forth to the music as I took my first drag of the blunt. I coughed hard from the harshness of the new wrap flavor. I tried the tantalizing pineapple. The smoke slowly faded away and I proceeded to finish the blunt with haste. My stress levels were beyond the norm for me. For a moment, I entertained the idea of quitting pot…HAH. Nah, never mind.

My 21st birthday came without warning in the middle of April. How did it arrive so soon? I never waited for it since I was lucky enough to have upperclassmen friends buy booze all throughout college. I thought about my weekend ahead. The fire department and surrounding emergency response non-profit annual gala was the day before my birthday. Although I didn't buy anything special for the occasion, I had my competition gown.

It was a bold shade of fire engine red. The silk material draped perfectly down my slender figure. The top was a cinched rhinestone detailed corset and the bottom flowed into a beautiful train. Looking in the mirror with that dress on made me feel like real royalty. My jet-black hair fell softly in curls over the sweetheart neckline. The gown also had a unique satin layer on top of the train that was like a men's coattail. It laid gracefully across any piano bench which worked well with my pageant talent being blindfolded piano. Vlad, Nadia, Natasha, Kathy, and I were to meet a limo at the hotel. Then Madison and her boyfriend would meet us at the gala. Since I was a public figure and it was my birthday, the fire department paid for my ride and stay. As a bonus, I was going to chair the event with an NFL Football Player.

I hung out in my bedding thrilled and anxious. My department only wanted me to say a few words and the pro footballer was going to do the lion's share of the talking…That didn't seem like a lot of pressure. A ping noise rang out from my cell phone.

Kathy: Hey birthday girl!!!!! HAPPY 21st!

Me: Thanks hon! I'm so excited. The gala begins at 7, but we should be at the hotel by like 4.

Kathy: Just grab me at 3 and we can swing up to Vlad and Natasha's to get them.

Me: Awesome! Make sure you wear your fancy wear :P!

We rode to the hotel and got unpacked in the suite I was gifted. Hotel Du Pont was a marvelous place, with stately architecture. The luxurious and imposing building overlooked the harbor in Wilmington.

"FUCK! I SPILLED CONCEALER ON MY GOWN," I shrieked from the bathroom. Vlad was visibly concerned while Nadia and Natasha rushed to my side with a wet cloth. My panic consumed the entire group. "This is absolute bullshit on what is supposed to be the best night ever!"

"I can get it off, Vlad go run to the ice machine" Nadia spat out nervously. The hotel that the department put me at was lavish and had a view of the water. Hotel Du Pont was the place to brag about amongst the upper class in Delaware. Luckily, they had all the things we needed being a young dumb group of early 20-somethings, including ice and white towels to remove semi-permanent stains.

My eyes shifted between the red satin fabric and Nadia. After five minutes of her elbow grease and iced water, I was relieved to see the stain removed. Checking the mirror before I left the bathroom, I was happy to see no marks and my sparkling state crown on my head. I walked into the living room to grab my banner.

"You're my hero, thanks, Nadia. Oh my God. I can't believe I'm freaking out over fabric; we have a party to go to!" I was so much happier in that moment and finally able to relax. The fire chief was so impressed with my donor recruiting, he wanted me to chair the event and speak on behalf of my experience as a volunteer. I successfully fundraised $10,000 for our department. It was the grandest night a 20 turned 21-year-old debutante could experience. The ladies only took a couple hours to get their hair, outfits, and makeup together. It was a formal event, so we sported gowns of different colors. I loved to rock red at fire department appearances. However, my friends went for gold, black, and silver. Vlad was the only guy in the group until Madison and her boyfriend came along to the event later that evening. Although this didn't bother him because he loved any excuse and opportunity to wear a tux.

Before we departed the suite, we all checked each other. My thoughts were running. It was disappointing that I invited 10 people to this amazing event to be spoiled and meet a pro athlete and only 7 of them showed up. I was dateless but kept a brave face and joked with Nadia that she was my date. It was so tragically funny and ironic that the same guys I rejected warmth from months prior did not want to be my date for my 21st. I can take some of the blame and credit for that. Some of my girlfriends comforted me by telling me it was probably intimidating for them – to have to share the spotlight with me. The struggle to find a committed date was real.

Nadia, Kathy, and Natasha all snapped me out of my self-pity party by showering me with compliments which at the time, I desperately needed. Most of us 21-year-old millennials were histrionic and sometimes in moderation, that's ok. We gracefully walked out and down to the limo to attend the prestigious ball. Arriving in style gave the night some fun flair. We walked in together. Hundreds of beautiful, vibrant red roses stood massively in a golden vase on a table next to a sign that said Fiery Night in fine script lettering. Dazzling gowns glittered across a sea of dimmed red and orange party lights. The time to get up in front of the 300 guests was approaching, when we walked into the lavish ballroom, I had about a half-hour to enjoy the event and then came my little speech. My friends scattered, treating themselves to dainty hors d'oeuvres and keepsake photo booth photos.

I decided it would be polite to approach one of the CEOs of the disaster charities who hosted the event. One's name was John and he was the leader of a nonprofit organization called Disaster Response Ops (DRO). While his teams did not often perform rescue operations as first responders, they served the field by feeding, sheltering, and clothing locals affected by natural disasters. He successfully recruited me to join his cause and I promised him he could give me a tour of the building and get me certified to be on one of his regional teams. The fire chief from my department was there and greeted me armed with two very cute little girls who were no doubt his daughters.

The air was so clear to me that night, especially as I looked around at the faces above the elegant beaded and crystal studded fabric. Smiles were all in sight including those on my friends' faces. Despite not having a date I was holding my own decently enough and socialized like a butterfly. It was getting closer to speech time when I walked to the bathroom to get in some last-minute alone time.

"OH!" the wind was knocked out of me and at the same time I was caught before even getting close to falling. Walking out of the bathroom I was staring at a nude on my phone sent to me the week before by Kristian. Looking up and shoving my phone into my dainty purse, I saw a bright blue-eyed, dirty blond hair stranger. He was tall, with an average build and neat hair, donning a tailored fitted black and white tuxedo. I quickly checked myself and adjusted my crown

"You almost lost your hat." There was something oddly charming about his corny statement that drew me in.

"Thank you," I responded with a somewhat meek and embarrassed voice.

"It's nice to meet you, Miss Delaware. I'm Calvin." Calvin said back in a less comedic tone.

"I'm Arie... and have to make a speech with that football player soon.... Um catch up with me later though because it's my 21st birthday and I'm here without a date!" wow I was such an idiot. That was the dumbest line ever – like oh hey, I'm a lonely, pathetic piece of crap, but your attention is totally welcome! I constantly overanalyzed what others were thinking. At that point, I wasn't sure if I would see him again since the event was so big and I made a total fool of myself.

When making my way up to the stage I saw the NFL Football Player with his wife, he was a doting husband and spoke so lovingly about his new baby. They were next to the stairs that led up to the podium. It was nice to break the ice before the big moment. We exchanged some pleasantries, I found out his name was Brad, but the moments flew. The announcer began calling us onto the stage to speak and one by one we made our way up.

"We have come here tonight to celebrate our volunteers, workers, and donors. We are also here, more importantly, to continue our life saving mission. Our duties across all emergencies and related disciplines…" I was inspired and impressed by how well the fire chief spoke to the crowd. He was dynamic, his tone was even, and he kept the crowd engaged. I took some mental notes, like the way he paused to emphasize what he said. This was his 15th gala with the department, so he was undoubtedly an expert at this. As a pageant queen, I should have been, but I was also an energetic 20-year-old with occasional stage fright. He finished speaking when Brad and his wife walked up to the stage.

"Every year, Brad and I try to raise and donate as much as possible to our fire departments and local emergency non-profit organization. We understand the trauma which can result from these natural and sometimes unnatural catastrophes." His wife spoke with such grace. She managed him well, and that was obvious through her interactions with him. He then spoke in his hyped-up athletic voice on the importance of volunteerism and making a difference every day in our community. The message was captivating but now it was my turn.

"When becoming a dispatcher," I began. "I was unsure what to expect and how I would balance it with school." I paused, thought on my feet, looked up with my eyes, and pointed to my crown. "...and work." The crowd chuckled politely. "However, what I have found is that when something matters to us, we make time for it. What the fire departments provide to Wilmington is beyond their rescue operations. They provide us all with something equally essential for a community to survive – peace of mind. Thank you so much to all of the brave firefighters and supporting volunteers who keep our city safe." I finished my short speech without a fumble. My friends were at a table close to the middle of the ballroom, but it was an awesome feeling seeing them applaud me. Having a hit speech made my night, but I wanted to find Calvin and stand next to him until he asked me to dance.

"Arie you did awesome," Vlad cheered. My close-knit crew walked up to me at the stairs next to the stage and podium. "You kept the crowd amused and kept it light too."

"Thanks, Vlad" I smiled and hugged Kathy, Natasha, and Nadia. "Before the speech, I ran into this really cute guy... well rather walked into him but it was a solid introduction."

"I'll be the judge if he gets to come back to the hotel suite with us little sis," Vlad said brother-like.

"Ha-ha be nice to the poor guy if he sees Arie again, she's a hottie with a body in a red gown with a crown.

Jade Greene

It's hard to miss her." Madison interrupted and emerged from the crowd with her boyfriend.

"Maddy!!! I'm so glad you and your boyfriend made it!" We hugged, and my friends greeted each other once again.

"Let's dance guys! The food and your speech were amazing, sorry for not getting to the hotel before Arie. Traffic was terrible." Madison sped through her explanation.

"Aw sweetie it's fine, you made it." I answered back in reassurance. Some of the group opted for more adult beverages while the others flooded back out to the dance floor, photo booth, and silent auctions. I went with the group going to the dance floor and was pleased to see he was there. Instead of waiting the anticipated half hour of standing around and watching him like a weirdo, he headed right to me in a striking and confident manner.

"Want to join me?" He smiled and must've been able to tell I was drawn to him. I nodded without saying a word and took his extended hand. We turned around and headed to the more crowded center, I gave my friends the OK and thumbs up sign behind his back, but I'm sure he knew I was gesturing to my friends like a child. He took my waist and hand as I took his hand and shoulder. As we enjoyed the smooth jazzy music, we conversed with one another. He made me laugh and told me details about his life. He was a 29-year-old astrophysicist who just finished his Ph.D. program. Prior to his master's, he used to be a volunteer firefighter for the department. In discussion, we meshed well together, and in the public's view, we became a sought-after socialite couple. Out of the corner of my eye, I saw a photographer nearby

56

take a photo of us dancing. I welcomed it without calling attention to Calvin as I was behaving, abstaining from alcohol technically being underage, and we were dancing tastefully.

My friends caught up with us an hour before the event ended. They all wanted to stay until the end which I was content with. Of course, my dopamine filled brain forgot I had a hotel room key and if I wanted to hook up with this real-life Professor version of Prince Charming, I needed to do it NOW. Everyone had a good vibe and was feeling the positive energy. Luckily, he gave me his number.

Me: Hey, want to head to my hotel room before the party is over?

Calvin: Let's wait until after we go on a real date and not ruin your sparkly image ;) though with your reckless behavior idk how it's possible you maintain it.

I looked at him with excitement, like the little nerd I was in high school getting asked to prom. Except I never went to prom or got asked. Ending the party was fantastic, they closed with a popular party line dance song, so all the older crowd got up to join in. The night was a dream come true, perhaps this year was going to turn around and I could change my life for the better.

My friends, Calvin, and I then headed back to the hotel room for my first legal consumption of alcohol. I smoked a cigarette with Vlad and Natasha. When we got done, I realized midnight was ten minutes away. It was a group decision to run to the terrace on the roof of the hotel with some champagne.

"10....9....8....7....6....5...." The group chanted like we were singing a song. This felt like something out of a movie, but it was real. Tears flooded my eyes because it felt glorious, a slow scene recorded in my memory that I'd hold onto and could replay anytime. Calvin gazed directly into my eyes "HAPPY BIRTHDAY ARIE," they all screamed and cheered as I kissed him. Our gang's arms rose to a toast on the roof of the Du Pont above everyone else in the city.

We cheered to our night and hugged each other. After, we went to the room to change, and we went to the bar. I was so drunk from a glass of champagne I forgot to take my banner off and just walked into the bars with my Miss Delaware banner. Surprisingly no one took a picture, and no one ever found out during my reign. Thank God. The night ended with me falling asleep alone, I don't remember much but my friends later recapped that Calvin hung out with them for a half hour after putting me to bed. God I'm such a lightweight.

CHAPTER 5

Attempted Arie Domestication

A few days passed when Calvin texted me again while I was studying on an early Tuesday night.

Calvin: What is your favorite restaurant?

Me: I prefer more casual vegetarian spots since I don't eat meat. It's not an ethical thing, just taste preference.

Calvin: Ha-ha that's interesting. So, you don't support PETA?

Me: Oh God no. Anyway, why don't I take you out? I recently became a member of The City Club, the most prestigious culinary spot in Wilmington.

Calvin: Oh God no. I'm taking you out before you take me out.

Me: Very funny. Ok, let's go to the Origami Swan!

Calvin: Oh…do they serve Asian food?

Me: No, the owner is just obsessed with the art of paper folding.

Calvin: XD

Calvin: Ok whatever you feel like doing is fine. Is 7 pm on Friday good?

I smiled to myself.

Me: That's perfect.

Calvin: See you then beautiful. I have to run home, eat and do some work.

While heading out from my room to the dining hall, Nadia approached me with a cheerful attitude. She thanked me for inviting her and gave the night a rave of a review. Pleased she reported she also got a phone number that night. We joked and laughed a bit at dinner. It felt like such a dream, but it was real that I had met a handsome, sweet, and educated stud.

"It's weird to be dating an older guy," I said honestly to Nadia.

"Yeah, but women seem to mature faster... plus guys in college are still immature." She replied frankly.

"Isn't that the damn truth," laughing so hard unaware of how immature I was. I knocked my purse off my chair. Clumsily I brought it back up to the table.

"I like Calvin, he seemed nice, and you obviously clicked with him." I blushed at her remark. For a moment his face flashed through my mind.

"He already asked me out on a date, he did it that night over text when I suggested we go somewhere alone," I told her with some hesitancy.

"That's interesting he didn't accept that offer, but Arie he's 29 and not 21. He's a more developed breed of dude than what you're used to." Nadia was right. I couldn't keep chasing frat boys for tail if I wanted a serious, public and monogamous relationship. The two together weren't realistic or compatible. We finished up dinner and headed back to the dorms.

The rest of the week was naturally a lull. I limited

my texting to once a day with Calvin and didn't call him as to not act too clingy or lead on that I was already crazy about him. He was empathetic but I could tell he had a smoldering side. He told me all about his cycling across the country to raise thousands of dollars for a cancer patient charity. I was impressed at how many countries he visited and back packed through on his own. Growing up in a comfortable family, I traveled to over 10 at that point, but never alone.

Studying was a struggle, but I coped by increasing my smoking without regard to how it would damage my body. I didn't really care, I just wanted to graduate in a little over a year and get the guy. Between Saturday morning computer classes along with an 18 credit a week schedule, I was overwhelmed and at the same time in some odd state of mania from meeting Calvin.

It was finally Friday morning and I was an absolute mess as I only had one class – gen ed. Women's Studies. It was one of my favorite courses but the professor wanted us to debate often. With this kind of pressure and my simultaneous excitement, I felt like exploding. Out of nowhere, before class, my mother called. She seemed to call more often when something was going on. It's like mothers attain a 6th sense upon the birth of their first child. So weird.

"Hey, mom! What's up?!" I answered joyfully while I walked outside to our dorm balcony and lit up a delicious menthol cigarette.

"I hope you're cutting back on your smoking," she clearly heard the noise of my flicking lighter.

"Mom I will after college, I'm so stressed about just getting through school with my test anxiety."

"Well ok sweetie, but it's not good for you. How was your birthday!? You only told me a little bit yesterday, you seemed to rush me off the phone."

"Sorry, I've been really busy and distracted this week. I met a cute and sweet guy at the gala."

"That's so nice! What's his name? What college does he go to?"

"He's graduated with a master's and just finished his Ph.D. He's an astrophysicist for the government. His name is Calvin."

".....I have no idea what that job does, but that's nice honey!"

"He's basically a super genius scientist, more importantly, he treated me like a real queen at the ball. He even danced with me!!!!" My speech sped up with my enthusiasm. I sounded like a bunny on cocaine.

"Ok, well I'll let you go, you know your mama just worries about you and just wants to see how you're doing." I put out my cigarette with some guilt and walked inside while she spoke. It was odd to think I was from that small town where my parents still lived in Ohio. Although I'd be lying if I said I didn't feel some regret for not visiting my family more. At this point, I was estranged from my father. With how horribly he and his conservative family treated me over pursuing pageantry, I feel any sane person in my shoes would've done the same. However, my mother was and will always be my best friend. She understood me and genuinely just wanted her children, my older sister and I, to be happy.

Class was a hodgepodge of unfocused energy that that room always produced. It seemed like there were never enough windows in it to clear the air after an intense two-sided debate amongst the class. We all got along, despite our different beliefs, and knew the ability to debate with logic and reason outweighed the temporarily awkward feelings we got from disagreeing with each other.

The day was lovely as I exited T Hall to walk back to my room afterwards and get ready for my date. It was 3:30 pm, and I had an ample 3 ½ hours to get ready. I decided on a healthy run on the treadmill followed by an unhealthy blunt on the balcony to calm my nerves. Balance, right? Even after wasting some time, I still had 2 more hours to kill. I ended up getting ready early and socializing (read: BRAGGING) around the dorms about my new boy toy. When my phone buzzed, I zoned out like a zombie in the middle of conversing with my friends.

Calvin: Hey Arie, I just got to your school, where do I park to come get you?

Me: The building's name is C Hall – I'm in the upperclassmen dorms

Calvin: Ohhhh look at you, Junior. Lol, I'll be over soon

Me: Sounds good!

My girls hugged me goodbye and good luck. At least if I blew the date, I had my sisters back at school to comfort me. It was nice to have such a large and loyal social group. The mirror nearby confirmed I looked good enough to go out on a date. Pleased, I put on my big girl snakeskin high heels and went out the door. Looking around as I walked outside, I saw Calvin in a custom trim, black Saab 9-5 Aero. The paint shimmered in the sunset and Calvin's hair was done the same way at the gala, tastefully combed with just enough taming product. He got out of the car as I got closer and walked to my side at the door. We kissed and as he pulled away his teasing scent lingered. Before my quick hands got to the handle, he did a half bow, opened it properly, and gestured me in. This was not the treatment I was used to, or even preferred, but it was still appreciated. He made me feel like an offbeat princess, and at dinner, we had some interesting ice breaker discussions.

"You think you're so much older than me," I quibbled, "but you still had Power Ranger figurines. You're a millennial, maybe an older millennial... but you played Sega and Game Boy too!!!" I teased so hard, and he finished swallowing a bite of his food.

"Ok, Miss gaming and comic book expert," he replied sarcastically. We laughed together. "So, what do you play and what are you into?"

"Well, the girls and I like everything I'm sure you and your guy friends like," I said earnestly, defending my interests as normal. "We play COD, ugh some of them play Halo, which I just cannot get with."

"No Halo!? I like both of those but am definitely more a Halo person." I could tell he was stunned at my knowledge.

"I mostly play WoW," I said in a hushed tone, with some embarrassment. The game was notorious for evoking images of obese greasy virgin men. Calvin began cracking up. I looked at him with a small frown.

"No, no, no, I don't think it's stupid it's just crazy that the most GIRLY girl I've ever met – you're a pageant girl… is into WoW." He fumbled a little. "Not crazy," he saw my frown stay glued on my expression. "It's refreshing you have a variety of different hobbies and talents. That's all, it's just rare and impressive."

My expression softened and I smiled at him sweetly again.

"That makes me feel better. I'm not a total nerd, I mean you met me at that fancy event." I said innocently enough.

"So, you're a nerd turned model then?" he asked.

"I guess…. though I haven't modeled quite yet. I only graduated from modeling school a couple of years ago and have been busy with college. I earned school through a pageant scholarship." I continued trying not to be too conceited. "I'm a little short for most gigs though. Most girls on the runway stand at 5'8+" I sighed. "I'm only 5'2".

"Well, you're beautiful and if you want to go do it, why not go do it – even if it's not runway?"

"I suppose it wouldn't hurt auditioning since pageants are much more short term than modeling."

"Is that right?"

"They're about the same for runway but not for print or catalog." Wow Calvin was letting me talk a lot about myself. I liked him so much, but I needed to know more. "What about you Mr. Genius of Delaware?" The things I said were so cringy, it sickens me sometimes. "What are you into?"

"Aside from science and games, I am a huge soccer freak. I play on our department's team. My passion is aerospace science, I work for NASA but most of the time I can be remote." He beamed, "but I still have physical goals. It's important to me to stay in shape, I love playing sports." He was so well spoken and mild.

"That's incredible. You're so balanced yourself. I like science, I have a lot of docs in my family but am much more interested in math."

"So that will definitely make our next date fun. It's nice we'll be able to discuss deeper things than what the new diet trend is." I smiled and frowned again at his remark. COME ON! Why are you menfolk so sexist?! Women are not stupid, shallow creatures only interested in makeup and what their boobs look like. I held my composure, but he could tell he got me and then struck a chord.

"I have a bunch of unique friends at DWU…. Not all women are like that."

"Many are."

"That's fair, but I'm a feminist so I don't like generalizations based off of gender, to be fair I try not to generalize men."

"I'm sorry Arie," his composure and confidence broke which oddly turned me on. "You're gorgeous, kind, and intelligent. I just want to go on another date with you."

"Absolutely. . . sorry I'm a bit of a contrarian. Heck, look at my mannerisms and where I go to college." I took a pause to reflect on my own rude behavior. "Sorry, I'm a little guarded, I haven't been abused by any of my boyfriends or anything, but I find it difficult to trust men. I get along better with women."

"It's funny you say that because I do too."

"Really?"

"Yeah, I can empathize with you, typical men are

difficult to get along with." He admitted honestly. "I see where you're coming from".

After we finished our meals and intense conversation, I went to the restroom. Like a gentleman, he paid the tab before I arrived back. He took my hand on our way out of the restaurant which shot electricity through my body. I had never been so infatuated in my life. Tension was running high in the car; I didn't want him to think I hated him after I was being a little ice queen at dinner.

Another issue that robbed my attention from him was that I desperately wanted a cigarette. The night of the gala, I told him I was a social smoker…As a reader, you're justified to laugh at me. It was common sense not to light a cigarette up in front of him if I wanted to be the perfect future scientist's wife. If any of the less conventionally attractive men deserved me, it was the best and brightest of them. City lights shined like Christmas decorations as we sped back to my dorms. Viewing the city's moving art landscape was enough to temporarily distract me from my addiction troubles. He smiled at me.

"I hope this isn't goodbye…I wanted to give you a tour of my place. Want to see where a genius lives?" He raised an eyebrow and smiled.

"Oh, I've had tours of my school a hundred times by now but thanks for offering." I smiled back. "Why can't I get that tonight?"

"Hahaha very funny. Hey, you're a beauty queen, model, and superhero genius…. I didn't know if you were busy tonight." He said frankly.

"Let's not waste time, I'm very attracted to you." My tone was more hurried. He jerked the car to a stop at a stop sign and turned his right blinker on. "No, don't turn around, I'm going to need my contact case, toothbrush, and birth control." He then continued and within a few minutes, we were back at the dorms.

Running through the halls Nadia tried to stop me. "Nadia! CAN'T TALK! GOING TO BANG A ROCKET SCIENTIST." In my room, I searched and found everything I needed for an overnight stay. Sprinting at race speed, I darted down the hall and out. As soon as I turned to the glass door area I stopped and slowly walked out acting as if this wasn't the happiest night of my life ever.

The drive to his place was relatively speedy since DWU was situated right next to downtown. He lived in one of the grandest condo buildings by the waterfront and marina. As an accounting major, I was perplexed and amazed.

"How can you afford this? You just got out of school!!!" I blurted out rudely. "Oh my God, I'm so sorry." He shook his head and smiled in response. I could tell he was proud of showing off his aesthetically pleasing space. We got off the elevator and walked to his place. When we entered his unit, I immediately could tell he was extremely driven in his field. In the corner stood a magnificent and high-end telescope, along with some drawings and what looked like research notes. He turned on his playlist and *Make Me Proud* by Drake started blasting. I was definitely picking up on his intentions. He started kissing up my arm to my neck and telling me how perfect he thought I was.

His touch was making me so naturally high; I wasn't even thinking about having a smoke. He pulled me towards him, both of our sleek bodies in his dark apartment with the windows open to the waterfront. We could rule this city's social scene. I caressed his face with my hands and lips. This was far more intimate than I was used to being with men, but I let my guard down.

"You can take me." I quivered as he traced the left side of my body with his fingers and cupped my rear end aggressively with his other hand.

"Will gladly do." He picked me up and brought me into his bedroom. While placing me down I started taking off my shirts, I wore a cute cardigan with a tight red camisole underneath. Calvin finished undressing before me and pulled off my jean skirt. I assisted in taking off my hot pink G-string underneath it. His parts were the perfect size, robust and thick, but not at all an uncomfortable fit. I pushed him down so that I rode him. Going on top became a habit because it was the easiest way to get off. I was in so much trouble. Looking at him I had a weird realization. He was the type that could calm me down and tame me if he wanted to. There was something about his presence that relaxed me and made me feel safe. I came at least 10 times within the hour we explored each other's bodies. We finished together and walked around naked. He grabbed some water and went into his bathroom to get his robe for me. I cleaned myself up awkwardly.

"Here you go." He said softly while handing both to me. I put his robe on and drank the water with a big post-workout gulp.

"I feel warm and fuzzy." I swiftly grabbed my birth control pill and drank a little more while swallowing it.

"I'm glad that you're responsible," Calvin said

as he picked me up off the bed and brought me to the living room. We sat on his couch and chatted for a few hours, him in his boxers and me in his robe. He was an only child who loved to play sports, travel, and plays video games. He also was an April birthday baby and I immediately brought up that we share a zodiac sign. We confided in each other. He told me that he felt his voice wasn't low enough to which I laughed.

"That's not funny, I'm being serious," he replied to my reaction sternly.

"I'm sorry sweetie, I just think it's cute when someone shows their vulnerable side."

"Well, what is your secret?"

"Sometimes…. I smoke cigarettes and pot." His face dropped. Internally I panicked, I genuinely hoped this wasn't going to come between us.

"How often do you do that?" He looked concerned.

"Daily," I said as calmly as I could. "I don't do it at events obviously, but it calms me down and helps me between my social anxiety in crowds and school."

"I still like you, but you should consider quitting. You know it's not good for you." He looked at me with a frown and blank stare.

"I know…I'm sorry." This was a horrible way to end the night.

"You don't have to be sorry, just consider it. I want my partner to be healthy and have a long life." He said sternly again. "Which prematurely leads me to ask – do you want to be my girlfriend?" My jaw dropped.

"Of course, I do," I responded without hesitation. Calvin was everything I wanted in a man, or at least I thought so. Appropriately, I warned him. "Just know that I'm a lot to handle." He smiled not understanding that I was being brutally honest. It was already close enough to midnight that I was content passing out with my new boyfriend.

We woke up and I grinned at him. He was facing the other direction, so I woke him up by giving him a soft back massage. He finally stirred and turned his head slightly. With one motion he was facing me and smiling. Next, however, he uttered something I had never heard after a fun evening romp.

"You need to brush your teeth."

I gasped, both mortified and pissed. Nevertheless, I knew how his type operated so I compliantly followed his wishes. I couldn't believe him, and on one hand, I was irritated. On the other, I was super turned on that this man had the temperament to dominate the Hell out of me. Coming back into the bedroom, still wearing his robe from the night before, I decided to get a little gutsy and go for seconds. The robe landed on his bed abruptly and I posed dramatically in the doorway. This easily drew his attention and uninhibited gaze of appreciation.

"Mine." He said viciously. I nodded my head in submissive agreement and sauntered toward him. The next forty minutes were spent on top of one another while the passion of fresh romance manifested on most of the furniture throughout his apartment. After, breakfast commenced with us on his balcony facing the complex's artistically designed pool and the harbor.

"This is lovely, and your apartment is so nice. Where are those photos on the wall from?" I inquired wanting to know more about my new sweetie.

"As you know, I cycled across America for cancer victims. So yeah, along the way I took those." My heart pounded with rigor. It impressed me to meet someone so worldly but young. He discussed in a storytelling manner, his journey across 18 different states and where the photos were taken along the way.

"You're so amazing." I said in awe.

"So are you, my dear," he said, kissed my hand and finished his food. We brought our dishes to the sink and passionately kissed for a few minutes…or maybe ten. I floated back to my car because I swear, I was too light to be walking. The fact that I didn't have Saturday class this semester made it all the sweeter.

The week dragged along as my junior year in university was coming to an end in less than a month. At the gala for the fire department, I met a former civil rights and feminist activist, Jennifer Dubois. She was a young 60 and a spectacular self-made philanthropic social justice warrior. She both invigorated and intimidated me, but I knew I wanted to grow up to become just like her. Shortly before running into Calvin, she had invited me out at the end of the month for a double date. She asked the week before our dinner date if I was single. It was a thrill to tell her after the previous weekend that I had a date!

The venue was something my young, inexperienced eyes had never seen. Even growing up affluent, children were not exposed to the adult lounges and bars in my conservative family. She and her husband set reservations for us at the most formal and exclusive business and social club in the city – University & Whist

Club. Calvin had a sports car which put my mind at ease because my little junkie Hyundai wasn't going to do for this occasion. He picked me up at my dorms where I flaunted my elaborate red Mac Duggal cocktail dress reserved for the nicest summer appearances.

"You are a vision, my queen." He was searching for something more creative, and I could tell but appreciated his stammering. "Hey if we're dating, can I call myself Mr. Delaware?"

"Don't stretch it, but maybe eventually" I teased and flashed a toothy grin. "I'm nervous, I looked this place up and I'm glad I did because I probably would have worn my short shorts and tank top or something."

"You get nervous about things so easily." He stated which dimmed the mood a little bit. Back to a topic that I did not want to discuss on the way to a five-star country club and dining establishment.

"Yeah... It's why I smoke. I love people but I get socially anxious and terrified of what people think about me."

"Wow, that's very good to know though."

"Let's change the topic. I don't want to spoil your already tainted image of me." I lit up a cigarette and he tightened his lips in sheer disapproval. He let it slide without a word seeing the stern reactive look on my face. We stayed silent on the way to the club, but I preferred that after the awkward exchange. Pulling up to the venue was like a scene out of some old world. It made me feel a strong sense of anemoia. Luxury cars lined the castle-looking building's parking lot and valets were rotating cars through the lot. We gave the valet our keys and headed to the doors. I put on my best professional pageant face.

Inside the club was expansive and decorated with various art pieces and oversized pricy furniture. Jennifer power walked in her Louboutin's towards me, but I heard her coming and saw her before I was hugged. It was obvious she and her husband had already started drinking. She was wearing a delicate midi-length gown that was reminiscent of 50's glamour.

"It is so good to see you future mini me." Jennifer slurred as gracefully as she could. Calvin was stifling laughter but quickly made friends with her husband Ollie who despite likely drinking just as much was in a more sober state.

"Well thank you, Jennifer. Coming from an activist titan like you, that means a lot." She was such a warm energy to be around. I hoped to age just like her, staying fit and looking divine even when I'm hammered. I loved how bougie the entire experience was. "Where are we seated?" I looked around at the lavish entryway.

"We'll be in the main dining room," Jennifer answered in a tipsy tone. The finely dressed hostess guided and sat us down. She explained the evening specials and I watched as Calvin politely placed his napkin on his lap. I did the same. I let Calvin order my drink for me. He chose an aromatic pinot noir that he claimed was the "healthiest" for runners and heart health. The men began their own conversation discussing the advancements he'd been working on through his job and program. Jen and I decided to focus on community service events going on in the city. I looked around after my second glass of wine and realized aside from graduating college and obtaining a career, this is exactly how I wanted my life to look. Although it was a little less than classy intention, I used the opportunity of befriending Jennifer to try to get a membership to this elite society. It worked and I became a junior member.

My logic was both selfish and humanitarian. Being able to help others was of importance to me, but I would be unable to make a real impact unless I became a vital, beloved part of the group of people who pulled city strings. With Calvin by my side, I had impressive, vetted, and handsome arm candy to become a married socialite with. We were the youngest in the club. The classic French windows provided a moonlit view from my seat.

Realizing the club was closing was a bittersweet moment for our little humorous unit. Jennifer hugged Calvin and I. Ollie gave me a brotherly hug and turned around to escort his feisty, and now absolutely plastered wife. I wasn't much better off feeling my three glasses of wine, but I was grateful Calvin abstained as the DD. The disagreement we had was effectively erased from a night of socializing, fine dining, and drinking delicious wine.

"Wow, I didn't realize you had friends in high places." He said modestly and I could hear the curiosity in his voice. The drive back to my campus was lovely with its moonlit backdrop.

"My father is a lawyer with his own practice. I know how to socialize in these circles. Then when I won Miss Delaware, I became estranged from his side. I still talk to my mother and most of my family, but even before pageants, I was used to finer things…and people growing up. Being a minority princess is awesome. It sucked as a kid in a whitewashed town, but looking back I'd take the bullying over the rapid aging some of them have had to deal with later in life." The little snarky bitch in my head howled with glee.

"That's mean!" He raised his voice in shock.

"Yeah well, I got bullied a lot by annoying, unattractive, and now to my smug satisfaction, poorly aging basic people from my small-town." I aggressively responded. Finishing with, "I don't feel sorry for them. I'm aware you're white but you need to consider my perspective from a childhood gaslit minority standpoint."

"I'm sorry you went through that. You have your life together, I guess I just don't see why someone like you would even linger over it." Calvin seemed to forget I was 8 years younger than him, and a little hard headed. It drove me insane when people assumed my gender determined that I was good at multi-tasking, listening, and feeling appropriate emotions at appropriate times.

"You're right." Realizing my foolishness, I calmed my own drunk ass down and discussed date ideas. Since finals were around the corner, I told him we can go back to my room. I snuck him in through the basement of the building, a typical upperclassman move to get some. Passing the doors Calvin inquired if I had a roommate. I was one of the fortunate ones who could afford a solo dorm. We had a quickie on my uncomfortable student bed, but it worked. It was hurried but efficient, since I was conscious of how little time I had to prep for my last round of junior exams.

CHAPTER 6

Broken Illusions

F inals were beyond arduous but by studying religiously, I carried on and got good grades. Luckily, I had also made living arrangements with Vlad and Natasha. Living in Wilmington over the summer was enthralling. I could travel up and down the coast whenever. They were thrilled to have me move in and at least have another income going towards the bills for three months. The only problem was I didn't have a job. I knew Vlad and Tash probably wouldn't kick me out, but I didn't want to let them down. While I was vacationing with my mother celebrating my 21st birthday, Calvin made an awkward dual confession. He was mentally struggling and missing up to 2-3 days a week of work regularly. Equally severe, his father and mother needed his regular financial help. The year prior, his dad was laid off from his company with thousands of others.

I felt stressed for my similarly disturbed counterpart. He was not seeking treatment for his depression, which made things even more complicated. I on the other hand at least had a therapist who wanted me to quit my vices but pursue a non-medicated path. Although medication is appropriate when it's needed, it's not always the right treatment. He needed to see someone to find out for himself, but it was damn near impossible to abandon him because I was falling in love. At the same time, I wondered if someone who couldn't even find an entry-level job at 21 could cut it for him in the long run.

The week before moving out was relatively calm compared to larger neighboring schools like Wilmington, UD, and DMU. Moving was horrible per usual, but all my belongings got to Vlad and Natasha's harbor penthouse. It used to be his mother's condo, but she got bored of it, moved out with her wealthy boyfriend, and let them keep it. Calvin let me stay over often, but as we were only a few months into dating, I didn't pressure him to move in.

Calvin: Hey girlfriend. ☺

Me: Hey boyfriend. How are you doing sweetie?

Calvin: Good, I wanted to see if you had plans with your friends this weekend.

Me: No, I don't, why babe, what are you up to?

Calvin: Me and the guys from work are going sailing tomorrow in Stone Harbor. Are you free? My coworker Kyle grew up there.

I accepted his offer and put my phone down.

"Wanna get a little high," Vlad scared me while mocking a famous stoner cartoon character.

"Jesus man, can you be any sneakier? And yeah, let's do it." Summer's quick incoming was evident with the sunshine beaming on top of the water. Vlad and Tash's balcony was decorated in an old Russian style. A gorgeous, elegant rug presented the circular top table like a pedestal. Two Pottery Barn chairs sat next to each other across from three folding chairs that were undoubtedly purchased for a party.

"What's wrong? You seem a little down man?" Vlad exhaled and said a little sloppily.

"I just hate that our culture," I said too fast.

"Your culture - I came over as a teen dude," he fairly debated.

"I hate that this culture revolves nonstop around work. We only have a limited time to do things and yet here we are constantly worried about work or studying so that one day we can work MORE!" I paused and spoke more about my existential crisis. "The irony is I love working, I did as a teen and do now but it's becoming more stressful with age. Like having a job that you like isn't good enough anymore. You have to have a job that makes a fortune, has benefits, a cool title, and leads to CEO at every company." I was despondent.

"You know you're feeling this way, not just because of culture, but because you're a first generationer. Bro, I know, it's a burden to maintain and attempt to grow the family fortune. Some of us don't even want to. I'm still making that call."

"You already have your degree. I'm just waiting for this bullshit to be done so I can move on and figure my life out. One more year."

"You got this man. Keep your chin up, you're Miss Delaware and so close to getting a degree. You'll get something good. You could always take a fluff job this summer. Why don't you try modeling?" Vlad responded cheerfully.

"Maybe you're right. Even if it's not an academically

relevant job it's something to pay my bills and who knows, have fun with!" I felt slightly better than when the conversation started.

The next day I went with Calvin to spend time with his coworker friends in New Jersey. However, to my surprise for someone who claimed to be "not like other guys," he fit right in in a disappointing way. While I didn't mind more masculine energy, I did not appreciate the misogyny and sarcasm my friends and I were met with. It was both mortifying and hilarious to me that Calvin, Mr. "I'm not like other guys" was just like if not worse than the other guys. I wish the narrative of sweet nerd was always law, but it seemed his group acted far worse and more disrespectful than any frat boy I ever met. I embarrassed myself further by bringing a couple of my single friends who were also annoyed at their blatant lack of emotional intelligence.

Leslie and my other friend Michelle became a dynamic duo. They were in the same class, below me but had different majors. We met because I decided they were cute and sat with them at lunch one day. While they were impressed with the guys that I was able to "catch", they were unappreciative of the sexism. We sat across from each other on the 40-foot yacht. It was bittersweet riding on such a luxurious vessel while trading our dignity for it.

"So, you're going to drop out of school and be a model? Smart girl you got here man." His one friend said stupidly.

"I never said that. I said for the summer I might audition to try to get some cash while I'm out of school."

"Leave her be man, she's just a girl. No need to tease her. That's my job." Calvin attempted to be flirty but missed the mark by a hectare.

The rest of the night was a blur as I decided to cope dangerously by binge drinking and refusing to eat. When we got back to shore, we went to a local bar. Afterward, Michelle sweetly volunteered to drive me back. Calvin was apparently "repulsed" by my "unladylike" behavior and didn't want to drive me. I didn't remember and woke up in my room at Vlad and Natasha's place hungover.

During my day of humiliating recovery, I looked online at upcoming casting calls, auditions, and agencies. Modeling school gave me some insight in terms of what to expect but I was naturally nervous. I fixed my resume up, downloaded my headshot, and emailed them out to some of the agency posts. Although I am short, I knew I could at least be a petite model with my body type and with the right brand. I spent the next several days working out and preparing for auditions. The entire time I avoided texting Calvin. The silence was mutual. I didn't let it deter me and was able to get my first booking after my second audition.

Me: I got a modeling job.
Calvin: That's good. Are you going to call me at all?
Me: Yeah, give me a few minutes.

Why did I text him? Seriously, I don't know why my dumb ass texted him, but I did. And ew, how opportunistic of both of us to use clout to attract each other. I didn't understand how detrimental to my health my new lifestyle was becoming. We briefly spoke on the phone to apologize to each other. I still wanted to make it work because he was wealthy, educated, and handsome. The checklist was complete and had added lines. It was decided among us that we were going to spend time together the next weekend.

Pretty soon after my first round of auditions, my schedule became full. I had to be at the next Miss Delaware pageant as the "outgoing queen" by the end of summer and between then was working constantly to afford my wardrobe for it. The gigs were straightforward photo shoots since I was a petite model and after a few go-sees, I got hired by a local modeling agency that contracted me often. My world felt even more glamorous but eerily unstable. It was convenient to get paid per shoot instead of biweekly and I at least felt comfortable with the images I was producing. I used it to escape while in a two-sided emotionally abusive relationship.

The next weekend Calvin and I had a quiet in-home date night. We watched a movie and made dinner. He was in a more pleasant mood and told me how proud he was of me for trying modeling. Unfortunately, the night turned sour when I went to change for bed. I discovered a pair of panties that were a couple of sizes too big for me in the empty dresser he allowed me to use. I stomped out to the living room and threw them at him.

"What the fuck are these? And what kind of ogre were you hooking up with behind my back," my face was turning red as I spoke.

"Arie, it's not a big deal. They're from my ex a few months before we started dating," he was lying. I knew he was because I had used that drawer for at least two months now and had never seen them. I left with my things and told him I couldn't guarantee that we were going to stay together. While my withdrawn behavior made him want me more, I was livid. I thought we were so in love, and I didn't know how this could happen.

I resolved to get revenge. My modeling agency was hosting a party the next day and instead of crying at home, I decided to go. Vlad and Natasha avoided discussing Calvin as they could tell I was not fully committed to the relationship. Without a word, I left my room head to toe ready in a tight little black dress. I waved goodbye and was out the door. The venue was at a beautiful art gallery in Philadelphia.

There were far bigger stars present than what I was used to. Delaware, New Jersey, and eastern Pennsylvania are all close enough to New York City that some of the local models were able to make it big. Some professional athletes and a few of their agents were present. I was ready for a new hunt and distraction from the drama with Calvin.

It did not take long before I was approached at the pop-up bar by a man in his mid-30s with striking black hair and dark intense eyes. He was an executive for a nearby football team and quickly accomplished getting my phone number. What a fantastic replacement, I thought. I discovered his name was Carson and he was 33, about four years older than Calvin. We drank and conversed easily which got my attention. About that time I craved a cigarette and I asked him if it was alright if I stepped outside. He agreed but shook his head.

"You're too pretty to smoke," he said.

"You're too old to say clichés and mean them," I replied annoyed. He got the hint and spoke again.

"Well, you are your own woman and despite your age, I'd say you're doing generally well. I just had an extended family member die of lung disease, so it's a soft point." He knew how to digress well enough.

"Wow…I'm sorry about your family. Thank you for opening up like that." His explanation was adequate. "When can I see your handsome face again? It's been such a fun night." I pined to be alone with him. He was tall, dark, and noticeably attractive.

"How about tomorrow? Let me pick you up on my bike and then we can have dinner. Don't wear a skirt though." he casually requested.

"I'm not riding on a bicycle with another person." I laughed.

"No, like a sports bike…a motorcycle," he put his face in his palm as he spoke.

"Oh! Yes, that sounds super exciting. I'm down," I responded naively.

The next day came quickly, and I threw on some skinny jeans and a cute black leather jacket. Carson came rolling up on a GSX-R1000 and I was turned on like a moth in a spotlight. He told me to take his extra helmet and secured it for me. I made sure it was in place, so I was prepared for the ride. Then we went off. He took a back road out of Wilmington to head to the country and zipped alongside a gorgeous stream. While waiting at a stop light he seductively looked over his shoulder and caressed my hand with his. I squeezed him tight. Eventually, we got to Pennsylvania and made our way back to the restaurant he wanted to take me to. While most of the ride was fun, there was a moment when he went 120mph and I whacked him on the shoulder.

"That was insane," I struggled to get off the bike while telling Carson my thoughts on the ride.

"Yeah, it's an awesome hobby. I started riding as a teen. My parents are both police officers and hated it," he informed me a little of his background which I was receptive to.

We walked into the Italian restaurant which had a rich aroma and relaxing tunes. The server poured us some water and Carson ordered some wine. He abstained from drinking since he was driving but wanted me to enjoy myself. I mentioned the normal first date details about me being in college and where I'm from originally. He did the same and added in the detail that he was Native American. As someone with Taino roots, I was pleased to hear we shared some culture in common.

"Do you need anything for your pageant farewell? If so, let me know. I don't mind buying beautiful women beautiful things." His question was met with confusion by me. Calvin didn't make as much but was well off in his own right and never offered any help.

"What? Like, be your sugar baby?" I teased and laughed. "You don't need to do that. I think you're hot anyway." I said quizzically.

"You joke but I like that arrangement. Women should be spoiled and pampered, especially ones as accomplished as you." He was lighthearted but serious. I was starting to really like this guy. It felt like I finally found someone who wanted to invest in me. Carson was giving Calvin a run for his money. Then to my demise, my phone went off. It was him.

Calvin: Hey babe I'm sorry about what happened a couple of days ago

I gave him the silent treatment and finished the meal. I agreed with Carson I could be his sugar baby with the understanding that we were open at the beginning. He told me to think it over to make sure I was ok with it and took me back to Vlad and Natasha's.

Calvin: Why can't we talk it over? I know I was an idiot.

I was so disillusioned from my experience with love, I did one of the meanest things a young "proper" debutante could do. I spent the summer dating both. If Calvin could play, so could I but I was still attracted to him and wanted to keep him around. I liked bragging about my "rocket scientist". While my behavior was promiscuous before, becoming a model made me downright manipulative and opportunistic. It didn't bother my conscience to take advantage of both. With a toxic version of feminism as an ever-present theme in my mind, I was just doing what men labeled "players" do to women. I was just better at it because I was self-aware of my assets.

Me: Yeah. We can talk. I'm willing to forgive you if you just admit you cheated. I'm not stupid.
Calvin: We'll talk about this in person.
Me: There will be repercussions to your actions, and I may or may not inform you of them.

CHAPTER 7
Double-Crossing Game

I hung my head in shame while walking into Calvin's building because I knew my weakness would get the best of me. Growing up in a wealthy household, prestige was a misaligned base expectation for me in romance. What set him apart from Carson or any man I knew personally for that matter was his brilliance. Calvin was incredibly intelligent, but he struggled with similar issues I used to grapple with. My narcissism was fantastic for attracting others but not useful in the long term. Spending more time in dedicated relationships, I neglected my friendships. What can you even say to a cocky, stupid 21-year-old that will change their mind or persuade them to act right?

He was frowning like a sorry puppy and gently approached me for a hug. I tried to slide him off.

"Come on my little ram. Let me love you." I wiggled out of his arms, walked to the other side of the room, and dropped on the couch.

"What was that? You know she reached out to me, right?" I asked curiously.

"I don't know. I was stupid. I wasn't thinking." He pleaded and tilted his head at me from where he was standing. After taking a deep breath and rubbing his temples he walked over to sit beside me. "Do you still want me to come to your farewell?"

"I do. Just be aware I had some choice words for your other girlfriend. Don't be surprised if she sends you screenshots, and I am not one bit ashamed of my domineering behavior." I shot back.

"What did you say to her?"

"Oh, I reminded her that I'm the alpha female here. I also put her in her place as I'm the one publicly on your online profile. She's not. I won the prize. She didn't and I win this verbal altercation because I win you."

"Did you say anything else?"

"I told her she was a hippo, and I knew right away her panties weren't mine because they could probably fit two of me." He frowned at my response as I curled my lips upward in a menacing smile. I knew that was an ugly moment of mine, but I felt all-powerful.

"You didn't have to be so cruel." He said as if he cared about her.

"You didn't have to cheat on me." I was still smiling.

"Fine. I admit we slept together but it was only once since we started dating. Just stop talking to her. You have me and I'll stop." He became dejected.

I decided to leave to give him space. On the way out I expressed that I forgave him. He gave me another hug and I drove back to Vlad and Natasha's.

It was a fault of my pride to take Calvin back, but I had barely forgiven him or forgotten what happened. By the next month, I had a serious boyfriend and a sugar daddy. I was disgustingly smug about it. By day I would hang out with Carson as he mostly worked around lunches and games. By night I'd look at the stars with

Calvin. Carson followed through with his promises as I was preparing for my farewell but couldn't attend it anyway.

"So, who do you like better?" Vlad asked me while passing me a joint. As usual Vlad, Natasha, and I were hanging out on the balcony. I had finally found some freelance work as a virtual assistant so I could work from home, have financial security outside of modeling, and be less stressed hanging out with friends in my downtime. Even with Carson's help I disdained the idea of me being dependent on a man.

"Calvin has the brains I adore, and Carson is very generous. . . But Calvin wins for me because of his mind. Maybe it's because my family is pretentious in terms of education."

"So is mine Arie but we both know school doesn't equate to 'intelligence'," he responded harshly.

"That's a fair rebuttal," Natasha weighed in.

"I don't like either of them." Vlad knew how to be a straight shooter of a friend.

"WHAT?! Why not?" I interjected.

"Dude. They're not good for you. They don't even come in when they pick you up and the last time Calvin came to party he sat inside and pouted." He was very serious.

"No, I get it. I'm never going to change for either of them. They both want me to change." I took a hard drag after speaking my piece and coughed a little bit.

"Just be single again. We miss you and you're never home." Natasha was half-joking and half-serious.

"Calvin's coming for my farewell. I told him I

wanted him there. He looks good in a suit." I laughed. My two close friends shook their heads at me in annoyance and humor. They were right though. More time spent consistently with these two meant less time with my friends. "Anyway, I have a date with Carson tomorrow." It was getting late and after we finished smoking everyone went to bed.

The next morning was beautiful, and we decided on a simple dinner date at his place. He owned a gorgeous house on the Delaware River in New Castle. I put on my newest little black dress and fluttered out the door with my night bag. It still was annoying me that Calvin cheated but what better revenge than following instructions from holy text? "An eye for an eye" was how I looked at our situation.

Carson bought me diamonds, gowns, furs, and photoshoots for my updated portfolio. I soon realized he, like Calvin, wasn't necessarily attracted to me as a person – he liked the titles and prestige.

I pulled up to Carson's house and strutted to the door. Upon opening, he flashed a huge smile from lips to eyes. He was the better looking out of my two guys by leaps and bounds. Carson was way more solid than Calvin. While Calvin's sleek soccer body was appealing to many young ladies, I preferred Carson's strong body.

"Hello, Arie." Something snapped in me, and I quickly moved my lips to his. We began making out and he sucked on my lower lip. I grabbed his sweet muscular ass, and he grabbed my petite waist to pull me closer. He interrupted me "hey, hey, hey. I have a surprise for you." This successfully got my attention.

"What? What'd you do?" I said bluntly. Like, spit it out man so that I can jump your bones RIGHT NOW.

"I made you chocolate mousse. On our last date, you said that that was your favorite dessert. I made dinner of course. You told me seafood, so I made salmon, squash, and rice too." He said sweetly. This surprise was so thoughtful, and I never had anyone make me my favorite food aside from my parents. I was grateful but taken aback by the gesture. I smiled and thanked him while smooshing my face into his chest with a sloppy hug. He walked with me to the table and pulled my chair out for me.

"You know this is..." I looked for the right words. How can you express such profound crushing emotions? "Kind and considerate. I'm sorry that I suck with words." He chuckled a little. We both enjoyed our meals, and I was surprised he cooked for me. This was something Calvin did not do for me, and Carson was wealthier. He could've easily taken me to the best restaurants along the coast but with my public persona I wasn't in the mood to go out. As an alternative, he suggested a few days prior that we keep this date intimate.

In a fit of passion, we ended up having sex on his car in his garage. He was also content allowing me to lean against it while fucking me. His grip on my waist was so hard he left a couple bruises. It wasn't his fault because I did bruise easily but his dominance turned me on. He took his dick out to rub around and tease me below. I begged him for more and he complied. He then turned me around and penetrated me again. I moaned and tried to stifle my volume. After the steamy sesh, we took a soothing warm shower and got ready for bed. We ended the night cuddling to sleep.

I wish I could say I invited Carson to my pageant title farewell but my young stupid self-invited Calvin instead. It was a ticking time bomb from the start. I knew I couldn't get away with smoking cigarettes or weed during the day. I dealt with it by getting an e-cigarette and occasionally sneaking out to my car to smoke late at night. Each day involved countless appearances at other age divisions' competitions and long rehearsals with the group competing in the miss division.

The truth is that while I enjoyed the process of enriching my life through pageant preparation, I hated the competition aspect. It seemed both frivolous and judgmental. Who cares if I smoke weed? Who cares if I bang chicks sometimes? I'm pretty sure Miss California was taking water pills to make herself look thinner through dehydration. Regardless, the industry expected us to be virginal, apex representatives of feminine beauty and empowerment. One friend once darkly termed it "passive eugenics".

We spent our off time wandering around Dover where the state competition was held. There were times in the chaos when I enjoyed being a respected young socialite with arm candy. Some days we went out without me wearing my regalia. On the days I did I was bombarded at restaurants.

"Oh my gosh! Are you really Miss Delaware?" A question from a nearby shopper. These moments were just getting weird – yes, I was Miss Delaware. Why else would anyone wear a banner? Gracefully, I met these questions with a smile and confirmed that indeed I was a pageant queen. Calvin would step up and volunteer to take a photo of the stranger who wanted one. At least everything publicly was so wholesome. We looked like the Kennedys walking around the crowds who were there to compete or support contestants in their family or friend groups.

It was the last night before I had to give up my title and I was a depressed wreck. I didn't realize the extent to which the title filled the void in my identity. Being 21 can you actually know who you are? My anxiety was getting to me, and I was out of weed. I was not going to make an hour and a half drive back to Wilmington for bud. Like many other girls on the last night of their "reign", I got booze at the local liquor store late at night after pageant officials went to sleep. I then proceeded to get mind numbingly drunk. We got back to the hotel and rode the elevator up to our floor.

"I am freaking the fuck out." I protested to Calvin. He was in a different mindset and expressed that he wanted some tender love and care that night. The doors opened and we arrived on our floor. A dimly lit hallway set an inappropriate atmosphere as we quietly made our way to our room. Once inside, the madness began.

"What's wrong baby? You look amazing, you have drinks to let loose, and you have me." He pleaded and tried to rub one of my hands. I yanked it away in angst and pulled my crown off. I was messed up but placed it on the desk to avoid it breaking in my tornado of depressive rage. Walking back to the bathroom my hazy brain started getting foggier. My temper was what prevented me from picking up drinking as a regular habit.

"Tomorrow I'm going to be irrelevant. You're not going to love me anymore," I cried and threw my earrings across the room irrationally.

"Christ. Babe, please calm down. I'm here for you."

"NO!" I shrieked in an irreprehensible tone through tears. He didn't even object. "You know I'm right. You like my titles. You like my relevance and YOU," my tone was rising, "AND NO ONE IS GOING TO LIKE ME AS JUST FUCKING ME". I slammed the bathroom door viciously and finished crying. My head was down when I walked out a few minutes after.

"That's becoming obnoxious. You can't drink anymore Arie! I'm cutting you off for the night." Calvin was blatantly unhappy. He knew that the press and anyone with a smart phone could get a recording if I kept going. I paused to avoid more disturbance as I did not want a bad reputation. "Look I do love you. You're so much more than your title. Come ON. This is kind of pathetic."

"You're mean." I didn't trust what he was saying and responded in an overly vulnerable way. I gave him a hug and two seconds later received a text.

Little Sister Queen: Can I stay in your room? My mom's being a bitch.

"Shit. Laura wants to stay over here." I spoke in a wavering voice. Everything was exhausting. The week was exhausting, the day was exhausting, and this transition was exhausting.

"You're not going to say yes?" Calvin questioned, visibly annoyed.

Me: Come on over boo. It's been a week for me.

The Miss Teen Delaware had some family drama I had witnessed at other events. I didn't want to say no, imagining if it were me staying in a hotel room with my father.

"You're a bitch." He relented and knew that I agreed. In ten minutes, my mini-me came to my room and we went out to my car. Calvin vehemently cursed me for smoking with my 18-year-old counterpart. We only smoked a cigarette each and headed back to get our beauty rest. It was nice to share an intimate moment with my friend. It was also sad to realize our connection would be gone in less than 24 hours.

The next morning, I woke up in an awful mood. Calvin knew not to bother me, so I decided to go on a short run while he slept in. I went out to run on a nearby trail for a few miles and returned to get ready for my last proud day on the job. Before the Teen and Miss Pageant finale, I hit up the salon to get a revamped look. They did big fluffy pageant hair and sent me on my way.

The show itself wasn't unusually remarkable. We did our production number which was an opportunity for the judges to get one last look at their finalist contestants. The superlative and optional competition awards were handed out. Then came our farewell videos. First, the teen went, and when her video finished her family came on stage to give her flowers and hugs for a job well done. Then the princess, pre-teen queen and I surrounded her with farewell gifts and flowers. Hugs were exchanged among us, along with tissues.

"We have another queen giving up her title tonight. For the last time, she is your reigning Miss Delaware, the first Latina in the history of the pageant to take the state's crown, Arie Casiano." The words "last time" stung. Then my final moment in the spotlight came. I picked up a part of my gown to avoid slipping on the staircase backstage. Stepping onto the stage and into the spotlight for the last time was so bittersweet. "I am the it girl…or at least I was." I thought to myself, bereaving my foregone reality.

My video played on a large projector screen next to the stage. It featured a montage of my year. I was a point of pride for the program and was notorious in the pageant community for my philanthropy. Additionally, my volunteerism gave me a name for myself among those in the nonprofit industry. At Nationals, I fell short in terms of overall score but won the Modeling competition and placed 4th in Talent. Tears flooded my eyes as I watched a past version of myself smiling at appearances and playing the piano blindfolded at nationals. While in my off time I was a party fiend, when I set my mind to work or hobby-related tasks, I got it done. My ambition knew no limits, so I began to feel embarrassed by my tears. I would not let this be the most relevant thing I did with my life.

The video ended, I received hugs and flowers from my family, sister queens, and Calvin. I did a final wave and walked off the stage appearing fine. I was not fine. My identity took a hard hit. When you're so immersed in something that you're obsessed with for a year straight, you become deluded into hoping it lasts forever. Nothing can last forever because we don't last forever.

CHAPTER 8

Distractions

Calvin was both angry and perturbed when he dropped me off at my apartment. Fortunately, my roommates were much more understanding of my melancholic mood. They welcomed me when I walked in the door with flowers and told me I'll always be their Miss Delaware. The sentiment made me crack a smile and we went about a normal day of hanging out and smoking together.

"Arie, we don't like Calvin. There is something wrong with him and he doesn't even seem to care about you." I listened to Vlad's words, accepting of them, but simultaneously upset that I spent so much time with this guy. A display of the sunk cost fallacy at its finest. "We just noticed the past few months you haven't been happy." Natasha nodded in agreement.

"I know you both are right. But I'd rather be in a toxic relationship than be single."

"That's not healthy," Natasha let out.

"I'm 21…is anything I do supposed to be healthy?" I was partially serious and partially joking.

With some distaste, we ended the discussion and moved on to simpler subjects such as the newest music produced by our favorite music blog. I closed the balcony door and carefully disposed of the ashtray ashes in the trash. The bed in my room was calling me so I pathetically slogged in and fell on it. Laying there, I thought aimlessly about the past week.

Carson texted me at least twice since I left for the pageant, and I felt some guilt for just leaving him on hold. I knew when I texted guys I liked, I couldn't help but show a uniquely overjoyed facial expression. For cis straight men who don't know if your girl is giddy on her phone but refusing to show you what about, she's probably texting someone she's having sex with.

While spending the summer distracted by the pageant and my new modeling gigs, I hardly noticed senior year was sneaking up on me within a couple of weeks. College was a reprieve where I could build my resume and be close to the big East Coast cities. It was an environment that fostered and developed my excellence.

It became clear to me that part of my anxiety was due to my codependency in my two relationships and lack of interaction with my friends. I decided to text Kathy.

Me: Hey man - what's going on?

I waited for a few minutes and was saddened to see a lack of response. Instead of pitying myself, I went on my laptop to check upcoming volunteer opportunities in my area. Disaster Response Ops (DRO) was a new organization created to assist first responders. When I met the CEO last spring, I didn't falter at keeping my promise and was so happy to follow through. Dispatching was becoming a little stale for me as the job was repetitive regardless of the call content. With some consideration for what the work would entail, I signed up.

It wouldn't be possible to hide from other friends forever, but my toxic distractions were my favorite coping mechanism. Not only that, but I didn't foresee either of my relationships going anywhere. If I kept up my behavior I probably would lose most if not all of my friends. Despite this, I wasted so much of my summer on the boys and learned that life gets bleak and boring without your buddies.

"I DON'T KNOW WHAT TO DO. EVERYONE HATES ME." I yelled into a pillow while walking out of my room. Vlad and Natasha were looking at me wildly when I pulled it off my face.

"…No, they don't. We don't hate you boo." Natasha offered sweetly. "Let's get out of the house and your mind off the boy biddies. Wanna go for a run?" She saved my life over and over without even realizing it. I nodded and gave her a ten-minute ETA for leave time.

We set off and enjoyed the gorgeous late summer weather. Delaware didn't get cold until mid-fall so many residents enjoyed all the warmth they could absorb before autumn. Running and socializing with friends should have been what I used to cope, but I was still immature. Natasha gave me some insight and told me that she and Vlad weren't worried about me. They considered me capable of so much and knew I could make my own decisions. She apologized for any offense, and I told her she was fine. It was nice to not have to worry about appearance and let my walls down for once. Things weren't so bad without a title.

The next week I caught up on texts, exercised, and rested. Calvin left me with a slightly bruised ego, and I overthought his behavior towards me. Carson was apprehensive to get together but understood I needed to take it easy. Spending time alone gave me the solitude I needed to think about my relationships. Carson was incredibly reserved and at least neutral with my friends, but nobody in my social circle wanted me to stay with Calvin.

However, at 21, I did not follow my rationality, I followed my curiosity. So instead of being rational, dumping Calvin, and trying a serious relationship with Carson, I stayed in the middle...stupidly. It wouldn't be much longer until the situation sorted itself out.

The second to last weekend before the semester proved to be mild. It was an easy Sunday that was speckled with clouds and light.

Calvin: Hey. Are you free later? You should come over.

Me: Yeah babe. When do you want me over?

Calvin: Whenever. I'm not doing anything.

I got ready within a few hours and was once again out of the house. The day seemed abnormally perfect, and the breeze was so calming. There wasn't much traffic. Families were either already at the shore for Labor Day or they were enjoying their last staycation before school. Hopeful and feeling more optimistic I made my way to Calvin's.

"Hey, baby. Missed you this past week." I said while opening the door. He was on the couch playing video games but saved his place and turned the console off.

"Hey. Come hang out. We should talk." He sounded upset which immediately set off my anxiety. I saw this coming but was emotionally unprepared. "I love you Arie, but I don't know how my family will react to you."

"So, we're breaking up?" I said with my heart in my stomach.

"Looking at my future I want someone that will fit into my family and social circle." He went on. "You're loud and conceited. You don't usually drink but when you do, you're insane. You smoke too much, you're intolerably vulgar and you're just too immature for me." He paused, noticing my tears.

"I've done so much for you. I've introduced you to several investors through my club. I even got all domestic and shit."

"I just don't think I could introduce you to my mom. Sorry Arie."

I left with a piece of my soul destroyed. The car ride home was long, and I decided to take some country roads to Pennsylvania. A mini road trip usually cleared my mind. Carson called me out of nowhere, so I awkwardly answered.

"Hey." I sniffed and wiped away some of my tears. Even I found myself to be very pathetic at this moment.

"Arie, what's wrong, princess?" His words soothed the aching pit inside me.

"I'm driving out to nowhere. Literally. I'm just driving. Can I be completely honest with you? I am not usually with most people." I hiccupped from crying, "but I want to be with you because you do seem like a good person."

"Well now I'm a little concerned but go ahead. I'm all ears babe."

"My old boyfriend dumped me. I feel like such a loser, and I'm SO UPSET." It felt like dead silence for at least a minute, but he spoke back.

"Well…thank you for telling me and as weird as this sounds, I'm happy about it. Not happy that you're crying but happy, because I really like you too. No offense to that idiot, but I want you to myself." Again, his words calmed me down. I finally stopped sobbing like a spoiled child. I realized being open and honest with guys wasn't so horrible.

"Thank you. I'm sorry for not telling you about him before."

"HAH I don't expect you to be the most mature or honest. You're a young thing, smart as can be but we all make weird decisions at your age. Why don't you go home and relax babe? We can hang out during the week since I work at night with the games anyway." I felt a slight tinge of embarrassment, but he was right. God, I need to figure this crap the fuck out before it hurts me.

With that, I turned around and made my way back to my temporary home. At least someone cared about me. I decided to spend the rest of the day sleeping. Unfortunately, the break-up was impacting me as my already thin figure was rapidly diminishing and I was losing weight immediately. Eating, hell anything, was difficult to do when I felt absolutely crushed.

In that last week, when each day passed, I counted

down the days to my last fall semester. Why was this impacting me so much? The idea of graduating was both exciting and disheartening. Sure, I would move on to my next phase in life but what about my friends? What about the people I spent the past three years living with? My mornings were filled with melancholy due to the break-up and Natasha and I facing our last year in college.

Additionally moving was a downright pain and challenge. My scholarship covered living expenses, so I was a dorm senior. I considered myself lucky to be spared from apartment expenses while I was in the semester. In a few days, I would take my belongings from Natasha and Vlad's back to school. Carson came over to pick me up on Tuesday for a date to the stadium he worked at. I told him I wanted to go on a private picnic, and he obliged in a quirky way. I was turning it on in the femininity department and wore a white sundress to show off my body.

I looked through the door window and he pulled up in one of his Mustangs. At this point he was doing so well he was able to buy a second one, the same year, same model, different paint job. I adored his extra, flashy taste. He was a goddamn prince. Opening the door, I teased him by trying to rub his black hair with my hand. He smiled beautifully and pulled his head away.

"You're a sight for sore eyes. White? Unique choice." He confidently stated once I hopped in. I knew the white would show off more than colored fabric.

"You look handsome…per usual." I looked into his eyes before he turned the car into reverse and took off. It was so easy to spend time with him because he was laid back. Someone like that could probably handle, maybe even enjoy a long-term relationship with me. His lack of temper gave room for mine to breathe.

We pulled up to the parking lot of the stadium which was empty due to the game being held the day before. There were only a couple of maintenance crew workers wandering around the giant halls. Carson wanted to show me a few hidden parts of it like where the locker rooms were for the players. We also walked pass the much smaller but charming cheerleader locker rooms.

"You could do that," he noticed that I was staring at the door.

"What, cheerlead?" I asked him. He smiled and nodded. "I used to dance competitively for years."

"I didn't realize I was with a triple threat. Dancer, beauty queen, and model? I'm done. Where have you been all my life?" His response was funny to me and elicited a good laugh.

"You're cute sometimes and former," I drew an asterisk sign in the air, "beauty queen."

It was just a funny idea. Who knows maybe with some time, I could revisit an old passion? While I loved piano more than dancing, I was oddly more talented at dancing. I think I chose that talent because I wanted to appear smarter which looking back was such a stupid assumption. We kept walking and finally came out onto the field. He had a table set up with some small sandwiches, pastries, and tea. While it wasn't a traditional "picnic", it was a sweetly received romantic gesture. The food was presented elegantly and tasted delicious.

"Did you get this catered?" I asked and stirred a couple of sugar cubes into my tea.

"I did! There's a tea house by my place so I just called in an order." He caressed my free hand with his and then kissed it sensually. His style of expressing intimacy was soft and more relaxing than Calvin's. The rest of lunch was chill, and we discussed our plans regarding our careers.

One thing that I am still amazed by is how productive he was. A daily routine for him consisted of waking up at 5 am, making his bed immediately after waking, working out, and working depending on if he had administrative or game-related events. He somehow would carve time out in between meetings and games to cook for himself. He loved cooking and found it to be a pleasurable stress reliever. With that, I casually mentioned that I wouldn't mind sexually experimenting with food since that seemed kinky. We discussed it before but this was more of a suggestion on my part.

"On that note – sweetie, you barely touched your food. You should probably eat something." He noticed my almost full plate with a handpicked scone and once-bitten sandwich.

"I know. I'll get my appetite back with time. It's been a crap week and I'm stressed about school." He frowned but didn't want to be rude and finished his lunch. Sunset was approaching so we made it back to his car and drove to his house.

He parked in his garage and opened my door for me. I slammed it and looked at him piercingly with a slight smile and head tilt. It had been a couple of weeks since I got laid so I was starving. Understanding exactly what I wanted, he grabbed me and picked me up. He then opened and kicked in his door.

"I know you said you wanted to experiment more with food. I have chocolate syrup and whipped cream." He spoke in between kisses.

"Yes. And to the shower!" I ran upstairs to his master bedroom while he grabbed the edible sex toys. I quickly stripped down to my innocent looking white lingerie and turned on the shower in his bathroom to get it heated up. He had a large steam shower with two shower heads.

"Hello, my little lamb." Carson appeared at the door with a few ice cream toppings. He set them down on the marble counter and slowly stripped down to his boxers in front of me. It was impressive to me that he was in better shape than even most guys my age. He had a broad but athletic build and was strong enough to hold me for long periods.

He took my bra off and poured a few drops of chocolate syrup on my nipples. The room was starting to steam so he pulled my panties down and off, then gently pushed me back and into the shower. After removing his boxers, he entered with me and set the toppings on the shower bench. I grabbed the whipped cream and sprayed some onto my lower belly, then my chest, and my neck. With a conviction to romance me he licked and kissed all three spots but stopped at the bottom on his knees.

I internally panicked.

"You don't have to do that." I hated oral sex because it felt too intimate and vulnerable. Nobody could get a closer look at my sacred lady parts than myself. "I'm not sure I even like it."

"I don't have to, but would you like me to have the

opportunity to try?" I trusted him and felt he deserved the honor of my spontaneous consent. I nodded and agreed verbally. He continued to kiss me down and started stroking me with his finger first. This helped me warm up to let him try.

My moans were so loud I was sure his neighbors heard us, but he assured me it didn't matter. I used some of the toppings on him after he got me to come. This was such an enjoyable session, and I discovered that I had a new kink. It was a relief he went with it. I kissed and licked off what I poured down him. Nervously I poured some of the chocolate syrup on his package and kissed it so there was chocolate all over my face. He rinsed his dick off and pulled my head up. Then he turned me around. I put a leg on the shower bench for leverage and let him enter me. Heavy breathing stifled my moans. After some pleasurable moments, he turned me back around to face him and picked me up. He pounded me so hard and displayed his strength in a fit of masculinity. We finished together as he held me up against the wall.

With a little pre-planning, our escapade wasn't as much of a mess as one would assume. We took a nap, but he had a game that night. He spoiled me with more kisses and attention. Very gentlemanly, he offered to drive me home. I thanked him with a long dramatic kiss and said that would be nice.

CHAPTER 9

Old Ways, Bad Habits

The start of the semester was as stressful as I had predicted. Moving was one thing but getting back into my normal social life after the whirlwind summer proved to be difficult. Deedee and Kathy distanced themselves for a reason I could never find out. My only guess was my inability to foster our friendships, but they could have called. I did later find out that Deedee transferred out. It felt like a sting only seeing a quarter of the same classmates I met freshman year.

On the bright side, Leslie and Michelle came back ready to party. It was a profound and needed reunion since our awful time with the wannabe astronauts. We spent move-in night in the floor kitchen playing cards and getting drunk. Instead of drinking, I smoked blunts on the floor balcony. We were so lucky with how the upperclassmen dorms were set up. It was child's play to get away with smoking and drinking.

It didn't take very long for the texts from DMU to roll in. Their move-in was the same day so surely there was teeming testosterone in the air a few miles away. The next morning, I woke up to a text sent at 2:30 am from Anthony.

Anthony: Hey Arie O :-)

"Am I going to ruin my potentially serious relationship again?" I said to myself while rubbing my eyes. I closed my eyes. "Yes."

Me: Aren't you dating some British chick?

He didn't text back immediately but at lunch, I received his response. It was obvious he spent the previous night getting blasted with his gang of delicious frat boys.

Anthony: I got dumped a couple of weeks ago. ☹
Me: Hey, me too! I'm still kind of with someone but you know how my crazy ass is.
Anthony: Come to our ABC (Anything But Clothes) party this weekend – it's on my page online.
Anthony: All your favorites will be there… Matt, Kristian Jake, and Andy.

I laughed at myself.

Me: Oh yeah…what did you hear from them?
Anthony: Pretty sure I heard half of it directly from you on the opposite side of the wall. Matt and I wanted to do a threesome with you.

My little heart fluttered. These boys spoke my love language.

Anthony: Come to the party. He and I will soothe your pain.

Me: Deal.

God, I'm the absolute worst. College to me was not a place where committed relationships were even possible. Who was I fooling? Also, let's be real, I'm dominant. When people with my personality are young and, in a rut, we get some D or P. I think I was more addicted to sex, specifically hooking up than I was to any substance. I walked outside and smoked a cigarette. Classes started tomorrow and I needed to get my ass into gear.

The first week of classes wasn't as bad as I thought it would be. There were some assignments and a few quizzes but nothing I couldn't handle. I discussed going to the DMU party with Michelle and Leslie. They were intrigued as they had only been to a few parties there in the past preferring to go out to clubs. We considered different outfit ideas since ABC parties were an opportunity to show off our bodies. They each picked a different material. Leslie opted for caution tape; Michelle settled for a hot pink duct-tape dress. I decided on a risqué two-piece number using only three bandanas. I tied two together around my bottom and one around my chest.

We spent the next few nights making our costumes and planning our shenanigans. Carson and I spoke a few times on the phone, but his schedule was getting packed with football season in full swing. This gave me a window of opportunity to misbehave in my favorite ways.

The weekend arrived after what seemed like a long wait. The three of us primped in my dorm and headed out in my car when we finished. We mutually agreed on playing hip-hop. I drove way too fast to DMU, and we rolled up like we brought the party. The house had a line out the door with all classes of students. We walked to the front of the line and Kristian was there.

"Oh, shit Arie. You know how to come up here." He pulled his unnecessary sunglasses down exposing his ocean blue eyes.

"You know it, handsome," I winked and smiled most slyly.

"Well, I missed you and your very lovely friends are welcome too." He waved us in. While we walked past him, he grabbed my butt, and in response, I grabbed his right back. I still had it.

All Night Longer by Sammy Adams was blasting on the speakers in the main entry. My favorite uni baseball team was moving up in their frat. Guarding the door for their house was reserved for upperclassmen. I walked up to the booth and saw Jake behind some ugly but popular shutter glasses.

"Where's Anthony and Matt?" I yelled over the bass.

"What's up Arie? And I think he's in the kitchen! You look hot as fuck. Swing by later." He gave me a compliment and useful information which I appreciated. I was an easily pleased player, and the warm welcome was wonderful. In the kitchen, Anthony was grabbing some jungle juice. He was sporting a toga-tied bed sheet. I walked right up behind him as he faced the counter and gave him a big hug. His back moved and his head turned to look behind himself.

"Oh well hello, Arie... and friends?" He was pleasantly surprised. He turned around to fully face me and I kissed him on the cheek. "I guess this one has claimed me for the night." He put his arm around me, and I politely stepped to his side.

"Michelle, Leslie, this is my favorite human at DMU and baseball player in the world, Anthony." I detached from him so I could grab a drink. It'd been a long time since I dabbled in group sex, so I wanted to be more mentally loose.

They each introduced themselves and I encouraged them to have fun. Although Anthony was no longer president, being in his master's program and having a presence on campus, he still had a hefty influence on the house. We moved to the living room and like a queen on a throne, I took my rightful place on his lap. The bandana covering my bottom rode up a little and I could feel him getting hard.

"Where's Matt?" I inquired curiously. He shifted his knee so that I fell closer to him.

"He's back at our place. He has a physics test next week already, but he agreed to a visit from you if you wanted to spend the night at our place." He spoke quietly enough that the roar of the party diluted our conversation. A beer pong ball landed on the skimpy fabric covering my bottom. I threw it back at a rowdy group of game participants. It was difficult to roll a fat blunt on his legs but I managed. "Want to go?"

"Let's hang out until the girls either pick their own boys or get bored," I whispered in his ear.

"Sounds good, country girl. Who came up with the bandana idea? Is that a flex at how in shape you are?"

"I totally did and yes." We got up and went to the basement where a different set of speakers were playing EDM. We got on the dance floor and attempted to dance. Instead, we ended up making out while taking breaks to attempt smoking my poorly rolled blunt.

"Get a room," Andy laughed as he walked around us holding Michelle's hand.

"As you get some bro!" Anthony teased. He and I loved encouraging debauchery among our friends.

"I love being with you." I looked at him pleasingly to express myself.

"You too. These are supposed to be the best years of our lives. Why waste them?" He answered.

"And we're on the last one." My eyes glistened woefully.

"We'll always be friends even if we can't be together physically," he said right before I kissed him again. He would end up being right. Years after graduation we remained friends. We had a closer bond than I and the other guys in his friend group. The jungle juice was starting to hit, and I'd only been at the party a half hour. I decided to text Michelle to gauge her attraction to Andy.

Me: All good? Will you need a ride tonight, cause if not I can take you tomorrow? I'm drunk so I'm probably staying at Anthony and Matt's tonight.

Michelle: Oh yeah. I like your friend, he's a hottie so I'm hanging with him.

Having enough of the strobe lights, sweaty atmosphere, and darkness, we made our way back upstairs to play beer pong. I told Anthony we should assist in breaking the ice with Leslie and one of his brothers so we could head out. He called over his friend Nate who I hadn't met before. I texted Leslie to come over and she walked in from the kitchen adjusting her caution tape outfit. We got a few rounds of beer pong going, smoked a couple more blunts and after we finished, I texted her.

Me: What do you think?

Leslie: Absolutely. Can you pick me up tomorrow morning though?

Me: Yup, yup. I'm drunk so I'm staying with Anthony and Mattie anyway. I'll get you in the morning.

We all hunted down our metaphoric trophies for the night and I mentally prepared to go to mine's dwelling space. I notified Anthony of this and right after 1:00am, we were heading out of the party. His frat brothers gave him the usual shit when walking out of the party with a girl. We walked a few blocks from the frat house to his and Matt's building. The excitement was building up inside me. I missed his familiar and cozy body. He was muscular, but I was already acquainted and comfortable with it. We got into the building, and he hurled me over his shoulder.

"JESUS. You're lucky I have boy short underwear on right now!" He walked to the elevator and plopped me back down.

"Yeah, but it's not full bottom. It's also see-through lace," he replied playfully, lifting my bandana a little. Oh, he was a good boy for paying attention and I was turned on. We rode the elevator up and when we got out raced to his apartment door. Though mid-run, I started skipping.

"Mattieee, we're home!" Anthony chirped upon entering his apartment. Matt came out of his room with a drink. He walked over and hugged me. "You look a little tired man, are you sure you can stay up tonight?"

"Today sucked but this," he went back in for a hug and motorboated me, "this is worth a study break. Did you guys bring pre-rolls or are you that drunk?"

"We're that drunk." I interrupted and pulled out my stash from my handbag. "We missed you though Mattie Wattie." I ground my bud as Tony went to the fridge for another drink. Mattie chopped up some of his Adderall and snorted it. He offered Anthony and I some, but we turned him down. I lit the blunt and spread my body out on their sectional couch. Anthony lifted my legs and sat my butt back down on his lap. Matt scooted over from the cushion that stuck out and lifted my head to place it on his lap.

It was my personal Xanadu, sandwiched between two young and stunningly beautiful male specimens. They knew how to soften my demeanor with the way they worshipped my body. Why settle for being treated like a queen when I could be treated like a sacred fertility goddess? I hooked up my music to their speakers and passed the blunt to Mattie so he could finish it. Anthony was rubbing the inside of my thigh with his right hand and my back with his left.

My drunkenness was subtly lifting, so I requested a beverage. Anthony got up and brought me back a screwdriver. With some masculine vigor, I tried downing it as rapidly as possible. Then the haze began to return. I started stroking Matt's chest while kissing him over his shirt and intentionally rubbed my legs against Anthony. This little lamb was ready to be consumed by my wolves. They carried me on both ends into Matt's bedroom and laid me down.

"What should we do to her?" Anthony asked Matt like they were in a hostage heist.

"Whatever you want I consent to. I actively do the consenting thing!" I was back to trashed and mumbling. Oddly I was still rational enough to not drive the girls home and instead spend time with two cuties I genuinely enjoyed being around.

"Let's play with her." Matt said with some darkness in his voice. "Sharing is caring after all." They started to remove my clothes as I enthusiastically allowed them to. I got up to undress them, but they were quicker than I was and both shirtless by the time I was in between them again. Matt had me from the front and Anthony played from behind.

"Mmmm, Mattie." I moaned in pleasure. I lifted my face to kiss Matt and Anthony got down on his knees behind me. While I wasn't a huge fan of oral, I had known these two long enough that I felt comfortable at least trying. To my preference, he used his fingers and not his mouth to massage me. After another half hour or so of increasingly aggressive foreplay, we were in bed together. Conveniently Mattie had a huge bed, which comfortably fit all three of us.

They began by taking turns with me. I lied between them and on my side to easily switch positions. Anthony was behind me again and sliding inside. I made a slight noise as the fit was tight. Matt was rubbing my front and kissing me while I held him intimately in my hands. I rotated to face Anthony while Matt took his turn inside. The night went extremely well, and we rotated between foreplay and intercourse for hours. At the end, I wiped myself off with a towel that Anthony gave me.

"You should stay over after that," Mattie called as I walked to the kitchen for some water. I returned to the room and posed at the door seductively.

"For sure…and I'm still a little drunk anyway after the double screwdriver earlier," I responded in my femme voice. Anthony was falling asleep, and Matt lifted the covers for me to get back into my spot. With a few bodily adjustments, I snuggled up to the guys and fell asleep. I woke up around 9 am but still didn't have texts from the girls. As I rose to look out the windows, Mattie and Tony stirred. Tony put his arm around me and pulled me down for more cuddles. I slept another half an hour and heard my phone vibrate.

Michelle: Hey, Leslie and I stayed at the house with Nate and Andy.

Me: Sweet. Did you have fun? Do you want a ride yet?

Michelle: No rush, the guys are awesome and hanging out with us now. Head over when you're ready.

I made some coffee for the boys and myself. It was convenient that I could smoke in their apartment. Although I couldn't light up a cig, I rolled a blunt and enjoyed my coffee on the couch. Anthony and Mattie followed me like two hungover zombies. Poor boys consumed way more substances than I did the previous night.

"I need to head out in a few to pick up my chickadees and drive us back," I touched Matt's chin with my thumb and index finger and kissed him on the forehead. "They're still back at the house."

"Ah, so they had an equally strenuous night," Anthony said and laughed tiredly.

"I suppose so. They said 'no rush,' but I'll get the scoop at lunch or dinner today, I'm sure. Nate and Leslie seemed cozy together last night." I replied. I went to the bathroom to brush my teeth and tie up my hair. Fortunately, I packed a tank top and athletic shorts in my bag. I didn't want to drive around in three bandanas. I kissed both men goodbye and agreed to party with them in a couple of weeks. Anthony informed me he started selling weed for fun and to smoke for free. Although he'd sell it to me at a normal price, I didn't mind supporting a dear friend's hustle.

I walked outside and down the street to the frat house. Before texting them, I grabbed my car from the street parking. The girls were glowing when I pulled up to them.

"Thanks for picking us up," I was greeted by Michelle getting into the front passenger seat. Leslie got in the back and graciously thanked me for the ride.

"Of course. I'm glad you guys had fun." I yawned and responded happily. They both proceeded to discuss their night, but the drive was short. We planned to meet at lunch, but all slept through it. However, we later texted to coordinate over dinner. I was pleased to hear Anthony's and Matt's brothers were respectful to my girls. This made it easier to go out and party with everyone as a group.

CHAPTER 10

Better Than One

Carson and I saw each other a few times the next two weeks. He was happy to see me but overworked. I felt sorry for him, but he explained that as exhausting as his work was, he loved it and it fostered his passion for sports. After spending time exploring nature on his bike, we started discussing more serious topics. These scared me further away from the possibility of monogamy. He wanted a housewife and a child or two. As old-fashioned as he could be, he fervently wanted to provide for a prospective spouse so she could focus on rearing his kids. It was such a shame for me. While I desired a potential spouse, I knew very young I didn't want kids.

My value system and attention span made me more suitable to volunteer for and serve families, instead of creating one. I loved kids, but as a minority woman, the expectation for me to have them was stereotypical at best and racist at worst. I wanted to be more than a statistic. Not to mention I was a shameless smoker and was self-aware to not entrap a man with a child and with my desire for wealth and status.

Classes were oddly easy compared to previous years. Maybe it was senioritis, maybe it was that most of my requirements to graduate were met, but I found myself with more free time than ever. The only thing I was nervous about was finding an internship for the spring semester. September was ending which made me hyper-aware of my limited time with my party gang and "harem". Knowing what I did about Carson, I should have called off the relationship but again – 21-year-old stupidity influenced me to selfishly hold on. Deep down I understood that I was wasting his time and like with Calvin I would inevitably fail at filling the mold he preferred for a lady. I never regretted wasting Calvin's time, but Carson was a big sweetheart, so the circumstances were different.

The girls and I planned to head to DMU's Frat Fall Fest. We spent another Saturday resting up and getting primped. Unfortunately, Leslie got a migraine, so she stayed home, Michelle and I headed out together. When we pulled up to park on the street next to their "Greek row" it was already getting crazy. My car dash told me it was 10:47 pm and the festival started at 10 pm. Students from surrounding schools as far as 20-30 miles away came to the party. We headed to the park where smokers were hanging out and food stands were set up. Andy, Jake, and Nate were at one of the benches. Jake stood tall while Andy was smoking a cigarette and sitting on the bench. Nate was enjoying what looked like a beer. Earlier, Jake had texted me, so we knew where to meet them.

"Arie, you said you were bringing Leslie," Nate said disappointed.

"I know I know. She's feeling terrible so give the

girl a break. We told her to chill." I said as Nate gave an understanding nod. Andy and Michelle were already holding hands in the two seconds that exchange took place.

"Well, we can still all hang out. It's always a fun time with Arie." Jake replied while looking over at Nate who was now the third wheel.

"Yo don't tell Leslie, because I like her, but I'll probably pair up at some point tonight or at least try. No offense to you, Arie, but I was hoping I'd see her." Nate said dissatisfied.

"I'm not covering for you, but I don't think I need to anyway. We're young. She likes you too, but homegirl is a third-year pharma major. She's busy." I stated and simultaneously made clear why she wasn't there. We went to watch the DJ stage set up in the school's courtyard a few blocks away and lost Nate. This wasn't a concern as he was a student there and we got that he didn't want to be a third wheel.

The night escalated and it was fun dancing with the guys under the stars. After a few songs, we moved to the bar closer to the park and the guys did shots. It was a fun and casual night. While I was feeling Jake and already getting in the mood, it was relaxing and lowkey to just hang out with him, Michelle and Andy.

"Hey let's go outside. I'm craving a cig." I said to get Michelle's attention.

"That works," she said and added, "let's hit the bathroom first though, I need to break the seal!" We laughed and walked off. After a trip to the ladies' room, we headed outside and left the boys to party. The dive bar we were at was inside a basement, so we had to walk upstairs and around the hallway to get outside. Once out the door, I fumbled around my handbag for my pack. I pulled a cigarette out and lit it.

"Can I have one?" Michelle asked innocently.

"No. They're bad for you and I don't want to be blamed for someone's bad habits." I shot back bluntly.

"I've smoked before, I'm not addicted to them and won't be. If I get addicted, I promise I won't blame it on you," she justified her question. While chatting we were interrupted by a plastered but handsome pair of guys.

"Are you guys from Wesley?" One of them slurred, clearly shit faced out of his mind. But he was kind of cute, so I entertained him with a response. It was assumed DWU girls were hideous butch lesbians just because we were at an all-women's college. It was also assumed that "hott" girls went to Wesley. He asked another question, "Can we get a ride back with you guys?"

"We're from DWU. Sadly, we're not ready to leave yet or I would agree to it, handsome." I tilted my head and spoke in a slightly bitchy tone. "What's your name? I'm Arie. This is my friend Michelle." I stepped closer to the streetlight and got a better look at him. He was a big guy, not perfectly muscular but athletic. His head was covered by light brown hair, and he had hazel-colored eyes.

"I'm Cole. This is my friend Brian." Cole introduced himself politely. Michelle was eyeing up Brian when she glanced over and saw me catch her. She looked at me and I stared right back at her as if to communicate, 'We can sample'.

"You both are fine. Hey, let's make out." My inner boisterous frat girl cheered out loud.

"I'm down," Michelle threw her hand up. We started making out with these two random cuties whilst taking a smoke break from our other two cuties we went out with. I'm sure there are some men with better if not equally great game, but guys who struggle, consider the lady's point of view too. We're not fragile, harmless little flowers. We're adults with sex drives who have egos and can be equally immature. Cole and I stopped, and Michelle and Brian were still stuck to each other.

"Bro come on we gotta head out. We have rugby practice tomorrow" Cole instructed his friend. Simultaneously I was thrilled to catch a rugby player. This was the type of athlete I was inexperienced with. He let go of my hand and asked "Can I at least get your number? After that, I wouldn't want to leave without it."

I gave him my number and Michelle finally separated from Brian. They were both more hammered than Cole and I. Before the boys caught a cab, Brian got her number and hugged her farewell. I assured Cole his fine ass would hear from me soon. I lit up another cigarette when they left and finally gave Michelle the one she requested a few minutes earlier.

"Hey, we thought we lost you," Jake was teasing as he opened the bar door with Andy following behind. I looked at Michelle and we burst out cackling. Fucking for feminism is awesome. Back then I had no issues covering for my lady friends but withheld that privilege from the guys in my life.

"Nah I'm just out here chain-smoking. You know how I do." I answered pretending nothing had just happened. Jake took the cigarette out of my hand and took a drag. "Let's move one more time and then head back to the house." Michelle had already texted me at the bar that she was delighted to spend another evening with Andy.

We finished off our night out with a nicer bar that upperclassmen frequented the most often. I avoided booze all night. It just wasn't my thing, but I didn't care what my friends did if nobody drove. Satisfied and tired we made our way to the house slowly. The night was relatively tame in comparison to my more recent bedroom adventures.

Jake proved to be a tender partner on his own without the chaos of the group influencing him. For whatever reason, the guys got more competitive and louder when they were in a group. He was far gentler being alone with me and we had an entertaining but peaceful night together. The next morning on the ride back to DWU, Michelle and I joked about what had happened. We decided fairly that that was an awesome once-in-a-lifetime pickup experience that we should take pride in. MIDDLE FINGERS UP TO OUR SEX SHAMING SOCIETY, was the mood in the car.

I dropped her off at the dorms and went to the park. For the rest of Sunday afternoon, I decided to go for a short run and apply for internships. As an accounting major, I wanted something applicable to my degree but unique. There were a few typical internships, but one stood out that was through the Philadelphia Federal Reserve as an investigative intern. I laughed to myself at the idea of pretending to be a spy. That'd be adventurous for sure but not what the position would probably even entail. To my surprise, I got an interview a week later and would start my position right after winter break.

Although I was still modeling there were some drawbacks to my new side hustle. Gigs could be bunched together in a week or scarce. Due to my height, I struggled to make it to the runway more than once despite my ongoing success in editorials and catalogs. I loved my body, but I didn't like that I was held back from additional work because of something I couldn't control. It wasn't something I could change with plastic surgery even if I wanted to. And I didn't. My height hindered me greatly in my early years as an aspiring model. Following petite and print-specific gigs seemed to be the most successful, albeit boring route for my job.

Mid-October Natasha and Vlad decided to throw a Halloween party. I was still unfairly grasping onto my relationship with Carson, so I invited him along. This time I went as a naughty catholic schoolgirl, and he went as a sexy professor. It was obvious to my friend group that my connection to him was problematic. After more time, he was either going to leave or retaliate as I was not behaving like a serious girlfriend which he eventually wanted.

He picked me up from my dorm and we drove over to my best friend's condo. Most of the party guests were already present and I rolled a blunt. He gave me a look of disapproval but left it at that without commentary. I came back inside to him playing the newest game craze – Cards Against Humanity. It seemed hilarious, so I joined in. A few rounds passed and we got up. We took a cute selfie and kissed before I went back out on the balcony to smoke a cigarette. Vlad came out with a ridiculous king-size joint and told me we were going to smoke it. It must have been at least a solid eighth of bud or more. Natasha, a few other party guests, and I without question were fine with that.

What seemed like minutes was an hour and I realized how crappy of a date I had been. I turned around and saw him sitting on the floor uncomfortably close to another chick and talking. She then whispered something in his ear, and he looked out the window back at me. Our eyes met for a moment. To say I was displeased was an understatement. The envious, all-consuming fiery rage built up inside the pit of my soul.

"Oh shit. Arie, that's Sarah, she's kind of a dick and notorious for poaching." Natasha saw me furiously glaring inside.

"I may be sexually liberated but I'm not an asshole. I don't mess with people in relationships out of respect." I replied.

"Are you taken though? To be fair you haven't taken him seriously," Vlad interjected rudely. My intuition was validated regardless of his opinion, and I got up from my seat. My red plaid skirt was crooked, so I straightened it, readying myself for a harsh verbal altercation.

"What the hell is going on here?!" I narrowed my eyes at this bitch. How dare she. As Carson spoke up, I turned my head to look at him.

"We were just discussing how she's also a model. She does runway." Carson answered in a drunken stupor. This statement made me livid. A strange feeling of jealousy bubbled inside me that I had never experienced before this. I could have punched that idiotic girl and Carson in the face for making me look bad. He hadn't drunk much during our card game with the group but upped his intake while we were outside lighting up.

"YOU," I roared at the girl. "Stop talking to my man or we're going to have issues," my eyes darted back to Sarah as I shamelessly yelled at them. "Carson get your shit, we're going back to your place, and BACK OFF you trashy cunt. I'm the alpha. You're not." Carson's facial expression was a mixture of utter shock and discomfort. He submitted to my barking orders and grabbed his coat while I apologized to Vlad and Natasha who were silent. "If I ever fucking see you, here again, don't expect me to be pleasant to be around," I shouted once more at Sarah who was in the corner sheepishly talking to her cousin who I met a few times before.

Carson was way too plastered to drive, and I was too furious. The entire situation was beyond problematic but at the time I preferred to make him drive. At least if we crashed it was on him, not me. My anger blinded my rationality and the entire ride home I screamed at him. If he had the dignity to mess around behind my back, I would've reacted differently. However, it was unacceptable that he hit on another girl, at my previous residence and best friend's party. It was humiliating.

"I love you," he murmured. This was not the first time he or I said it to each other. The statement only fueled my irate fire.

"SHUT THE FUCK UP. I'M TALKING. NOT YOU," I shouted. By the grace of God, we somehow made it back to his place without destroying his car or getting pulled over. We walked inside and I went to his fridge. Upon opening it in a mentally unstable place I found a bottle of champagne. I drank the whole thing while the next few hours of arguing ensued. "This is too much; no wonder so many people wait until after college to seriously date," I thought to myself at some point in the heated exchange.

I'd love to say we kissed and made up that night but that's not exactly what happened. We did make progress and get to a talking point. He did literally get a kiss from me, and we started cuddling, but I was still red inside. It wasn't so much the betrayal; it was showing dominance over me in front of my main social circle that gave me a deep-seated grudge.

It would have been a great opportunity to break up, but I clung harder despite his actions. The next morning, I went back to school in full-on revenge mode. It was a cool and calm fall Saturday morning. The smell of decaying leaves and the cold air felt cleansing on my face as I walked to my dorm building from the parking lot. I pulled my phone out.

Me: Hey hottie.
Anthony: Does my favorite duty call?
Me: Yes. Can you hook me up with some green and can we hook up?

These days, it's hard to imagine bud being illegal but back then you had to get it through dealers or friends. Times have changed for the better.

Anthony: Come on over. I can take a study break.
Me: Sounds good. Give me a couple of hours. I was out last night and look rough.

I ate a granola bar and chugged a bottle of water. How I avoided a hangover made zero sense. Maybe adrenaline from the rage indirectly alleviated the symptoms. Getting ready provided a nice coping mechanism and catalyst to calm me down. By the time I left I felt and looked much better.

When getting into Anthony's apartment I gave him a quick kiss on the cheek. He and I were hanging out more with me being his customer. I would often ask myself why we weren't dating. Ideally, I would've loved to be a "thruple" with Matt and him. They could share me, and I had a sexual appetite for them both. They were also uniquely different aside from their individual gifts of large endowments. Anthony was much taller than Matt. Matt had dark brown hair and the darkest eyes. Anthony had big blue eyes and naturally black hair. One was more bookish, and the other was more athletic, but they were a perfect pair to me.

Matt was knee-deep in homework so after a quick hug and brief hello, he retreated to his room that we spiritually desecrated only a month ago. Anthony had more time to just hang out. We smoked a couple of blunts and I confided in him about Carson. He listened respectfully without offering advice and instead of giving me an encouraging pep talk.

"I'm glad we're both single this year," Anthony joked. "Or um... I guess sort of single with your situation. Are you going to dump him?"

"After a while, yeah. We don't want the same things." I took a drag of the blunt after replying. I shifted topics. "What about us?" I asked sweetly.

"What *about* us?" Anthony replied. I looked at him and thought about it for a moment.

"We could try a thruple thing." His eyes widened and he rubbed his head at my words. He then proceeded to laugh but stopped realizing I was being serious.

"Arie we both come from a white-collar, educated society. You know the expectations. Get married to one person, buy a big ass house, and have 2.5 kids." While what he said stung slightly, I knew he was right. He had no idea, but I'd later fall in love with him and never would have the audacity to tell him. My toxic commitment issues were undoubtedly tarnishing the glitz and glamor of my debutante stud life.

"I know you're right." My tone lowered. I frowned a little and Anthony scooted closer to me on the couch.

"We will probably stay in each other's lives. You know… after all this. We're still friends." He glanced at his books on the end table. My heart was full. "If you wanted commitment, you know I'd probably take you on like that." He kissed my forehead and brushed my hair back in a silly way on top of my head. "Don't act like you're even ready for that. I know you're not."

"I know and at least you respect our differences. You're going to make your future woman or women happy." I replied by teasing him and leaned my head on his shoulder.

"If you're not in the mood for it don't feel pressured. Breaking up or getting ready to do it is stressful."

"Can we just cuddle then?"

"Yeah baby." This felt more like cheating than intercourse ever did. My energy buzzed and my heart was content being vulnerable.

"What makes you happy?" He asked gently.

"Weed." I was blunt.

"You know what I mean. What makes you happy in a relationship?" He directed my head towards his for a kiss on the lips. It was pain relieving.

"At this point, someone who just accepts me."

"Then don't settle until you find that," he rubbed my arm. "Have all the fun you want but once you're ready to settle down, find someone who doesn't judge you." He smiled in a response to my smile. "We're young babe. We have a long time to figure that serious relationship stuff out later. Whoever ends up with you will be a lucky guy too."

"Thank you." After a few more kisses I got up and gave him the money for the bud. He gave me a fat bag and an all-encompassing, warm hug. He put his head on top of mine.

"Everything will be fine. Don't let the media or society rush your life," his words were unusually wise for our circumstances, but they were well received. "You're enough the way you are."

CHAPTER 11

Baby Steps of Maturity

I gave myself the next week off from boys and did another catalog modeling gig. I also trained to volunteer for DRO. My dispatcher team was sad I was leaving but understood at my age I wanted to try new things. I signed up for DRO's bulk distribution and disaster relief positions. For distribution, the tasks were straightforward – unload heavy boxes off of trucks in communities that needed the supplies they carried. Disaster relief was more involved including minor rescue missions, disaster assessment, and setting up operational shelters when housing got destroyed.

"I should just resign my life to the Peace Corps. Society is so boring and empty." I thought adamantly to myself. The thought of giving up my material possesions to serve a higher calling intrigued me.

In the last week of October, I was right back to my old ways. It would probably take a miraculous humanitarian deployment for me to chill the hell out and focus on doing good in the world. Time was speeding by, making the sight of clocks and calendars discomforting. After graduation, I needed a healthier set of hobbies than getting laid and smoking. It was an odd mental transition period for me and my habits. Fortunately, my cigarette habit lightened up. Being surrounded by friends again made it easier to keep my smokes away in my purse. I also realized that during my spring semester I wouldn't have as much time to party with my internship.

Halloween fell on a weekday and everyone in the city celebrated a few days earlier. I decided to avoid Carson after my embarrassing display and instead texted my newest target. Regret still permeated my mood and through some reflection, I realized how hypocritical I was. Granted we did not share the same values and were not compatible long-term, he didn't deserve that.

Instead of my schoolgirl costume, I settled for a cute 70's one to brighten up my cloud of emotional defeat. I'd never been to Wesley but wanted to give it a chance. The previous week Cole invited my girlfriends and me out for his rugby team's Halloween party. The normal routine commenced with Leslie and Michelle getting ready in my dorm and us taking off in Betsy.

Me: We're heading down. See you in Dover handsome!

Cole: Hell yeah! Look forward to it.

When we got there, it was evident that the campus was done with midterms. Apartment balconies close to campus were lit up and packed. A few bars around the city had lines out the door. Still, we laughed at the cornfield of a town because we were so used to hopping around bigger cities. The small environment was charming though and we were excited to be there.

We walked up to the address and through the door since it was already open with other party attendees passing us. Hip-hop was blasting inside and almost immediately Cole approached us.

"You three look great! Glad you could make it." Cole welcomed us. Donning a zombie costume, his clothes were tattered and he was covered in fake blood. He scanned all three of our faces and then glanced down at my costume. "What can I get you to drink?" He walked us into the kitchen which connected to a larger living room where most of the party-goers loitered.

"I'll just take water. I have these anyway," I stated matter-of-factly and pulled out a couple of joints. A small change I started to make was switching from blunts to joints – any effort I could make to eliminate tobacco from my life was worth trying to me. Michelle found Brian who introduced Leslie to one of his handsome friends. Brian was shorter than Cole but had nice lips and exuded charm. Their other friend, whose name I later found out was Roland, was tall, handsome, and perfectly black. Rugby players seemed a little thicker than my usual baseball boys.

I had no complaints and enjoyed the fantastic unobscured views of their phenomenal behinds. They had all the typical party attractions, a buddy DJ, beer pong, and other drinking games. I pulled Cole aside to a corner and the trusting boy had no idea what he was walking into. Resolving to balance the sexual behavior I wanted to try getting to know him before hooking up with him. I wanted to be open and who knows maybe find someone I could be sexually rebellious and crazy with!

The conversation quickly took an awkward turn when I asked his age.

"18," he said adorably while I proceeded to cough uncontrollably and drop my joint. I was both mortified and hit with guilt. Ugh.

"Wait so you're a freshie?" I asked and he could sense my concern.

"Yeah, what class are you in?"

"I'm a senior." My face gave away my feelings.

"That's not that big of a difference," at that age, it kind of is. I had already been through the bull of freshman year and learned how to navigate the sexually charged, sharkish dating waters. He was innocent and I was at my most jaded. I didn't want to stay long. He needed to be on my turf if I was going to break him in and be real with him. I texted the girls.

Me: We need to leave

Michelle: Why? You guys looked like you were having fun!

Leslie: Arie I swear to God if you're robbing me of an opportunity to hook up with this dude, I will be SO MAD. >: - (

Me: Girl I'd rather drive my ass back down here tomorrow than stay. Cole is 18. My mission tonight is OFF.

"Who are you texting?" Cole asked me. I spent a few more minutes digressing to other topics. There was no way I could do this whole "open and honest thing" here, in a foreign place... with a teenager. Wow, I was an idiot.

"Just the girls. Ugh hey, I'm sorry about this but I'm getting a bad migraine. I'll be back tomorrow morning to pick up Leslie and Michelle though. Let's plan something up at my school in a week or two."

Leslie: ... Are you sure? I can give you gas money tomorrow. I'm probably going to stay if you're serious.

Michelle: OHH Arie's robbing the cradle! Does he know you're an older woman?

Me: It's not a big deal and no need. It's my fault for not asking over text.

Me: Michelle WHATEVER. I'm only 3 years older than him. It's weird but he seemed cool with it.

Michelle: I'm staying too. Sorry, you're feeling weird.

"Aw ok. I hope I didn't say anything wrong or creepy. You're really pretty and I want to get to know you." He was so sweet. My internal titans were in a full-out war. I may have been deviant, vain, and sometimes delusional but I was not someone who took advantage of a teenager. If he wanted some, he could fully consent to what he's getting into in a sober mindset, after full disclosure was given and he made the effort to come to me. I didn't willingly or intentionally break people's hearts.

On the drive home, I considered how I was going to improve my toxic behavior. It was embarrassing that I got to this point. There were moments of feeling divine and heartbreak on the emotional tightrope I was walking. I could feel both at the same time if the circumstances permitted. Hooking up wasn't the problem, my dishonesty was. I was playing the wolf in sheep's clothing game which was eventually going to lead to more humiliation and harm. Shame started to kick in. I put on some music to distract me and pulled out a cigarette. Questioning one's life meaning and value set makes time fly because it didn't seem longer than ten minutes until I was back in my dorm, alone.

I went to bed and the next morning picked up the girls before Cole had a chance to come out if he was still at the party. They were more than happy to share details about their crazy night and like a good friend I listened. There was no reason to let my mood ruin my friends' so I seldomly confided in any of them. I think the only reason I did with Vlad and Natasha was because we lived together. I couldn't hide from them. It was a consolation prize to at least see my girlfriends happy. Little did they know, I was emotionally and morally disappointed with myself.

Carson and I went on a few dates over the next month and things went back to normal with our relationship. Every passing day gave me more anxiety. Soon I would be starting my internship and college would be over. I wasn't going to let it spoil my opportunity to have a fulfilling adulthood but seldom are we humans motivated by the long term.

Deedee started talking to me again via text, but Kathy was still MIA. I'd occasionally see her between classes, but she commuted. This meant that I didn't run into her as often as my other friends. I guess the silver lining is that I could self-actualize through the poor decisions and consequences. My social circle was unraveling but that happens when graduation is looming. People are ready for the next phase and excited for "real adulthood" to start. I had a future but inappropriate feelings to accompany it.

After my failed attempt at nailing Cole, I decided to throw my intimate party in the dorms. As a freshman, I did it more often. With experience, I realized I didn't want to clean up and would rather go out to party. I took advantage of any excuse to enjoy my friends before we had to leave school. The theme was lingerie – the men were encouraged to strip down to their boxers or bring robes. I only invited him, Brian, and Roland along with my two loyal party pals.

Michelle, Leslie, and I went on a walk since the day was particularly warm. The last leaves were falling, and the trees looked bare, but the sun glistened through some minuscule clouds. We went to a spot on our campus behind the park and smoked a couple of blunts. Michelle and Leslie started drinking. One would wonder how all three of us achieved high grades and one of us would even make the Dean's list every semester. Anytime we were in our dorms, we studied. All the pent-up competitive tension led to us coping through typically horrible, youthful habits.

After loosening up we were ready to party. We got back to my room and the girls got dolled up while I cleaned up enough to not look disgusting. The boys arrived a few hours later and we brought them upstairs. While we had a curfew for male visitors, none of the students took it seriously and with an equal opportunity mindset, it was unspoken but fair to everyone. Students who were into women could go undetected. We knew at some point we had to walk outside with them to appear like they were going home but could sneak them back up through the elevator in the basement.

The party began with the six of us playing Kings

(also known as Ring of Fire at their school). I decided to drink because I was comfortable in my dorm and knew I wouldn't have to drive. The boys were fun to be around and complimentary towards us. They were also curious about our life at an all-women's college. We explained different perspectives on it. I had a scholarship and wanted an environment where I could focus but be close enough to a city where I would still enjoy my experience. We were polite and asked them about Wesley – all three were freshmen and buzzing about the ~*~newness~*~ of the college experience. The discussion was endearing.

In the middle of a round, I got up to prepare a hookah I borrowed from my suitemate. Knowing this could be hazardous I attempted my best to explain the basics of it to the boys. They'd never smoked a hookah which back then was all the rage. Although my freshman year was spent at the local hookah bars, again with experience, I realized it was cheaper and equally fun to just hang out with friends, host, or attend someone else's party.

Not ten minutes later we had an incident and luckily, I was prepared with ample first aid supplies. The conversation kept up with the drinking and out of the corner of my eye, I saw Cole make a dangerous rookie move.

"This is so cool Arie," he reached his hand towards the coal chamber as he spoke.

"COLE NO!" I shrieked and it was already too late.

"Shit. What do we do!?" Leslie whimpered as we all watched him get up and run to the sink in my suitemate and my bathroom. Cole was yelping in pain, and I knew we could get kicked out of the dorms for smoking in there – even if it was just harmless hookah.

"I got this, don't worry," I spoke with stoicism. You must remain calm when someone else is hurt or in an emergency. It reassures them and helps prevent the person from panicking. Even if a situation was dangerous, panicking only made any pain worse. "I got you, babe. It's ok." I grabbed my first aid kit and calmed him down. I shook up my spare cold pack and told him to compress it on his palm until it felt frozen. Then I set the faucet to lukewarm to help it heal. It didn't help everyone except me was blasted. I was playing the game with beer; they were all playing with liquor.

Leslie and Michelle reacted out of necessity and disposed of the coal by running it under cold water with the tongs in the hallway sink and throwing the wet pieces away. After a couple of minutes of Cole ice packing his hand, I rubbed some burn ointment on him. He sighed and expressed his agony. Roland and Brian watched in shock but continued to sip on their beverages. In case the RA heard Cole I requested they hide the hookah in my largest desk drawer which was mostly empty aside from a medium bong. We were lucky she didn't hear us because she never came by that night. If she did all three of us could have lost the ability to graduate with the school's rules.

"Look you're probably going to wake up with hella blisters tomorrow which sucks because I know you're an athlete." Cole looked saddened by my words.

"Am I going to be ok? Will I be able to play rugby this week?"

"If I were you, I wouldn't play until you go to a

doctor Monday to make sure it doesn't get infected. If it's not, you can drain the blisters. Don't rip off the skin, just pop and drain them. Don't cover it with band-aids either, use gauze on this. That'll heal you up quick and you should be ok by the end of this week." I knew this advice through firsthand experience. When I was 16, I was working alone at a coffee shop and closing the store. I pulled out a coffee strainer while it was roasting which sent a cascade of 450-degree coffee down the back of my right hand.

I felt so sorry for him but at least I was able to wrap him up. Once the ointment was absorbed into his skin, I put on a numbing cream that would help him feel better.

"Wow thank you Arie…. I've never had a girl nurse me back to health."

"Don't sweat it. I'm sorry that happened." I said but felt so guilty. To be fair, I did try to warn him before it happened. "You guys can all stay in here tonight. Let him get some rest when he's ready to sleep." Still drinking and somewhat quiet, the boys nodded at me in agreement. "Anyone need a cigarette after that craziness?" Everyone said yes, so we took the party onto the upperclassmen's balcony and decompressed from the chaos that ensued prior.

On the bright side, the stars were visible, and the night sky was clear. It was a little chilly but that was expected for November. The girls were coming down from shock, so the group dispersed to get some talk time with their guys. Cole and I stayed in the center of the balcony and sat on the bench. I sat there realizing how stuck I was between virtue and frivolity, decadence and purity, universal right and universal wrong. God this sucked. Couldn't I have one more evening of excitement before cutting him off? Regardless of virtue, I did anyway.

"That was very nice of you and kind of hot." Cole laughed and looked into my eyes.

"What? Me helping you with your hand?" I inquired.

"Yeah. I've just never seen a girl do that." His response made me chuckle because I had known at least a few personally who did.

"Oh. Yeah, I don't know. I love animals *and* people. It's a natural reaction for me to just help when I see someone or something is in need. I volunteer often when I have time to." He looked starstruck. Really? Over this? I just found it funny because I felt everyone should have that innate sense – it's a survival reaction.

"That's awesome! You just do it – most chicks do it for their resume." The comment irritated me, but it was not Cole's fault he was ignorant of norms in the nonprofit world.

"So... I have a reply for that. Even people who volunteer for their resumes, they're still good people doing good things. It just happens to be a win-win for individuals." He furrowed his brow, and I went on to explain. "Only 7% of Americans currently volunteer at all. If a volunteer needs an extra pat on the back, participation trophy, or words of praise, I'd still rather have to do that than not have them. We need all the help we can get and it's more hands to help others." He looked down and back to me then nodded.

"That makes sense. Huh, that kind of makes me feel weird. Maybe I should serve some organization too. I used to in high school" I smiled at his sincere sentiment.

"Absolutely. Find a cause you care about and see how you can help. Also, I need to say something to you now…I'm not a good person."

"What do you mean you're not a good person?" He asked, taken aback.

"I'm like every other horny college student, young, dumb, always trying to get laid and stupid. I just don't want to take advantage of you."

"You're not taking advantage and you're so tiny and harmless." He laughed at my fair concern. "I'm fine with this. I promise. I won't catch feelings, Arie." He rolled his eyes, and I took his words seriously. I then rationalized with myself that I gave him another warning… If he chose to burn himself again it wasn't my fault.

"Let's go back inside cutie, it's getting colder." I motioned the girls back inside and they brought Roland and Brian with them. The night ended as my old in-dorm parties tended to. We all successfully hunted our targets and fooled around in my room. My beds were pushed together since I had the room to myself. I turned on some Krewella and all 6 of us got on the bed.

There was no intermingling this session because everyone was already sloppily hammered. Cole probably stood 6'1 but he weighed at least 190-200 pounds. He was built like a sexy thick heavyweight fighter. The next day Leslie told me at lunch she was amazed he didn't crush me. Lingerie and boxers covered my floor. I had to be careful and stay alert to Cole's injury so I didn't hurt him even more. After we finished, as couples, we all cleaned up and went to bed.

The next morning sucked as they left. Leslie was

exhausted and had a blast with Roland. She practically floated off to her room – I did similar after spending time with my DMU boys. Michelle knew something was off and asked me what was wrong. I told her my plans of cutting him off and she was disappointed.

"But why? He likes you and out of all the dudes I've seen with you he gave you the MOST undivided attention. Not to mention he is your type… huge and packing."

"Exactly. I'm screwed up enough as it is on my own. I'm not getting entangled in anything serious with him and negatively influencing his life. He deserves a classic, well-behaved Becky who is content just hanging with her man. You know that's not me." She listened intently to my rant.

"So, when are you going to do it?" She asked with some concern in her voice.

"Today. When he gets back to Wesley and texts me."

"That's rough dude. Good luck and I'm sorry. If it doesn't bother you, I still want to see Brian."

"Girl, it doesn't bother me." I gave her a confused look. "Just do you. I'm over here just trying to clean up after my demons who make monumental messes of my social and romantic life."

I waited patiently on the balcony and chain-smoked. Baby steps. I can only give up one or two bad habits at a time. It's not like I had unrealistic expectations or a desire to join our college's convent. I bargained with myself. If I did the right thing today with my personal life, I could sort out my other problematic behaviors the next day. It took one brutally grueling step at a time.

"I'm going to do the right thing. I'm going to do the right thing. I'm going to do the right thing." I anxiously repeated this mantra in my head to myself. An hour flew by, and I heard my phone.

Cole: Thanks again for fixing me up, Nurse Arie. I hope you weren't too serious last night. Cause I kind of do like you.

"FUCK." I screamed out loud. Nope. I needed to do this and get it over with or I was going to hurt this kid. For his sake, I needed to end this now. I waited for him to text again. I walked inside because I knew I could get in trouble for screaming profanities on campus. My inner succubus was telling me to continue playing.

"Come ONNN Arie. Where is this shit even coming from? When did you all of a sudden become a picture of morality?" She bemoaned my efforts to change.

"Don't listen to her. How many times has she gotten your hopes up for love? How many times have they worked? Don't you want to openly love and be loved?" my inner crusader fought back.

Cole: I'm finally back at my dorm and the guys made it to their places.

Me: Look I need to tell you something.

Cole: So do I… I wanted to know if you'd like to be my girlfriend. You made me feel special last night.

Jesus Christ. Why couldn't I have done this to a tool bag Chad? Or Calvin? He was making this difficult for me. I felt so bad about what I was going to say but I knew it was the right thing to do, fully aware of my flaws and intentions.

Me: You're a freshman and I'm a senior. I need to tell you how this is going to go. I'm going to graduate and you're going to have three more blissful years of this.

Cole: What are you saying?

Me: I'm saying that I'm jealous af of you. Also, as much as I'd love to say yes, I have to say no. You need to enjoy this. You deserve to have fun without being tied down.

Cole: I don't understand.

Me: I don't have good intentions and I don't want to hurt you. The only way to consolidate those two realities is if we avoid dating. Honestly, I don't think we should see each other at all. You're looking for a girl. I'm looking for my identity which I can't obtain through a relationship with any man.

To my relief, his disappointment turned into anger, and he got rude.

Cole: Well fine. If you won't date me, I'm going to find a prettier and better beauty queen!

I visually imagined him slamming a door at me and audibly stomping away. "See Arie?" I mentally reassured myself. "He wasn't for you at all. Let him be young." Although I still felt guilty for hurting his feelings, it was better than him falling in love with me and me crushing his heart with my infidelity issues. Maybe I was polyamorous. Maybe I was a swinger. Maybe I was just a narcissist with a God complex. It didn't matter because this was something I needed to figure out and resolve on my own. A man couldn't "fix" me, but perhaps I could do some self-maintenance and find a new way to fly, without running into others.

People assume when you want to change it just magically happens, yet they wonder why it's so hard to be healthy. NOTHING worth having changes or happens easily. Relapse can happen outside of chemical addictions and nobody including myself is perfect.

I went to the dining hall having felt like I just got the crap kicked out of me. Leslie and Michelle were there with Nadia. We hadn't partied much with her this year because she proudly started the school's musical theatre club with Madison. Maybe instead of partying that weekend, I'd go see them perform. That seemed like a proactive way to support my friends' passions.

"How'd it go?" Michelle asked and visibly cringed.

"Well, it's over and it went. I'm sure Roland and Brian will give you two details. He wasn't happy but I was honest with him." I was silent for a moment. "Nadia, how's your musical going? Are you guys going to put one on before the end of the semester?" I just wasn't in the mood to talk about partying or boys. Lunch was chill and we just talked about other topics. It was a refreshing break from the billowing snowball tumbleweed hybrid that had become my messy sex life.

CHAPTER 12

New Year and Era

Most of the students avoided partying before finals because it wasn't feasible with a full-time course load. While I did have a few more exhibitionist adventures with my baseball team at DMU, I didn't feel bad because the arrangement was mutual. They knew what I was doing, I knew what they were doing, and we surprisingly developed complex friendships out of how we operated. Most of the time I would request alone time with each of them, the other times, we had fun as a team. My consciousness at this point was back to my other habits.

Winter break was terrible, and I hated separating from my friends. I hated leaving my comfort zone, but it had to be done for me to grow up. I came back before the spring semester to take my last gen-ed during the winter term. It was an art class where we had to make the materials we were going to use to create. This was another opportunity to cope while trying to quit cigarettes and enjoy my last winter on campus. Anthony and Kristian did something similar and signed up for classes during the winter break.

The fun and magic of what we did behind closed doors was still there, but I didn't need to go out targeting unsuspecting "victims". To these boys, I was a beloved fluffy "house pet" and as someone who fully loved the pet play kink, this was an ideal arrangement for everyone involved. No power plays, no lies, no pain, just lots of fun.

I should have done this sooner and just been honest, but something inside me loved the thrill of the hunt. It was sometimes nice having an empty campus to unwind on. My schedule was only going to condense with my upcoming capstone class which included my internship with the Fed.

Still, I was determined to squeeze out the last bit of fun. I could tell the foreseeable transition was getting to the guys too. All of us were only taking one class each so we could hang out more randomly. The second week in Kristian and I had a conversation that I remembered. We were hanging out at his dorm.

"What are you doing after school Arie?" Kristian poked my arm while asking.

"Hey, what's with the poke?! And oh...Hell if I know. You seem to be ahead of me on that."

"Yeah, but I'm still nervous. The Ph.D. route isn't easy even if it's a way to have something set in stone." It was lovely to see this side of him. I was on the opposite side of the couch rolling a blunt, but I finished up, crawled over on all fours and curled up next to him. On this occasion, I wore black rhinestone encrusted cat ears. "God Arie, you're so damn distracting. Why don't you just stick with modeling? You have the experience."

"Modeling is a hobby." I looked up at him and put my legs on the back cushions while hanging my head upside down like a little kid. My cat ears fell off. "Looks will fade anyway. I want a real career that's lucrative and does some good in the world." Being upside down muffled my voice.

"Well, that's a start and you're almost done with the bach."

"Am I ever going to see you after this again?"

"Yes." He stifled laughter and nodded his head. "You will. I trust you wouldn't intrude on a future love interest…and you're my friend." I think most people hate that phrase. I felt it and I loved it. Kristian and Anthony showed me that month that love does not have to be romantic for it to be healing or "count".

"I'm excited to say, 'I knew him before he was on the Science channel'!" He smiled and knew I was flirting.

"Well, I'll say the same about you when you go out there and do something incredible. You already have. It's just going to get better. Don't worry so much about "losing" college. Your real friends like me will always have your back. Plus, you're not *losing* anything. You're GAINING a degree."

"That's a good point." I paused and reflected on the statement. "You're right handsome." Mutually beneficial open friendships were the right thing for me during that phase in my life. I didn't have the same issues of developing feelings for them that were unrequited. I know a couple of them caught feelings for me, but due to our differing aspirations, it was what it was. Over time relationship related boundaries of staying separate became the unspoken expectation among us.

We were holding each other at this point. He wasn't the brawniest, but he was the most creative of the group. He had soft blue eyes and cute, unruly light brown hair.

Although he majored in chem, he had hidden talents that made him so endearing to learn about. He could play the piano beautifully and as a musician, I loved that about him.

He kissed me from my lips down my chin to my neck. I bonded with him on a more emotional and mental level but enjoyed his lanky and fit physique. We both started feeling each other, moving downward and began messing around. His dick was thick and felt amazing sliding inside me. I pushed him down and crawled on top of him to mount his sexy body. While riding I came at least 5 or 6 times. After switching to doggy style, he finally came. All the comfort he gave me might have been in vain, but he kept his word about remaining in touch with me after graduation. He held my hand and softly tugged on it to follow him. I decided to spend the night since he granted me a wish to be vulnerable.

I was finally finished with my winter semester and volunteer training. DRO had volunteers serve locally before deploying on national or international disaster ops. It was the last week of winter break for standard schedule students. Since I started my internship orientation and semester the coming Monday, the timing was convenient to get my first experience on call. We worked with the fire department but unlike dispatching, we'd assist with recovery efforts. The first fire I responded to was heart-wrenching.

I was in bed when I got the call in the hellishly early hours of the morning. The automated voice message system told volunteers a summary of the emergency. It also included the address, number of families impacted, and whether there were fatalities. I was relieved to hear "no fatalities," in the message. Practically falling out of bed I crawled and then walked to my dresser. Putting my uniform on I looked in the mirror.

"This is my new era. I'm going to be a better person." I said to myself in the mirror. My hair looked awful, but I couldn't worry about appearances with an emergency at hand. I grabbed my go pack, ran to my car, and drove to the local chapter. It was not exciting to drive to the chapter in my car. It felt like an added burden. Volunteers in my area were to obtain a vehicle for both anonymity and safety. Each car was an outfitted SUV, suitable to enter terrains impassable by standard cars. I picked the Suburban since it looked the safest. Security handed me my keys, told me to return them with gas, copied a photo of my driver's license, and had me sign the waiver.

I ran back out to the parking lot feeling my heart pounding. It was a single-family fire that was 15 minutes away but that doesn't make it any better. Knowing someone's home could be destroyed felt horrible. I learned that morning that I needed to shut up more and do better for my community.

The scene was not difficult for me to find. Firefighters were still packing up their gear. The front windows of the house were broken – a common occurrence for first response and sometimes a necessity to put out a fire. My heart sank. My partner was already on the scene and to my relief he was a much more experienced volunteer.

"Hey. I'm Arie." I introduced myself in a disheartening manner. "What happened?"

"Nice to meet you, Arie. I'm Patrick. I wish this

meeting were under different circumstances." He looked up at me from his clipboard and ripped a sheet off. He handed it to me to read and instructed calmly, "This was a fire, but we don't know what caused it yet. We still need to speak with the person impacted. The fire investigator already spoke with her, and she seems collected enough for us to go in. First, we will inspect the damage so that if the utility company, landlord, or insurance company require hard evidence – we have it for them."

"Ok. Do I need my helmet for this?" I asked dutifully.

"Absolutely. I haven't been inside yet, but from the outside, it appears to be major damage." His words struck me. There were a few ratings below major, but major meant the house was unlivable until repairs were done. It was barely a level below destroyed, which meant the house was unlivable regardless of repairs. He continued, "After that, we sit down with the family or person (in this case person) and we interview her to see if we can assist any further. Your training should have gone over this."

"It did," I answered quietly. You can train in a classroom or gym for weeks or months, but nothing prepares you for your first call to an emergency. "Let's go." I put my helmet on and fastened the strap on it.

We walked past the firefighters, and I thanked them for their service. Pat led the way, and I entered the glass shattered front door behind him. The inside of that house still haunts my memory. It was damp and smelled like burnt garbage. A housefire smells a lot like a bonfire except with the presence of burnt plastic. It's like a nasty chemical stench that meanders unwanted.

I walked through the living room and immediately noticed a turned-over bookshelf. The books were all destroyed and waterlogged.

"Watch your step. Depending on what happens, the rating could change." I stepped into the kitchen first and looked around. There was a basement door that was burnt hinting at a bad furnace. Pat walked into the small room with me. A few seconds later the floor we were just standing on in the living room collapsed. I jumped back deeper into the kitchen and further from the clearing.

"Let's leave. It's still major but it's no longer safe to be in here." I nodded and we walked out the back door in the kitchen onto a solid cement staircase leading to the fenced-in backyard. We walked to the front of the house and informed the fire chief what happened. He agreed the structure was still repairable, but not currently safe to even inspect. The chief informed us that the renter or homeowner needs to contact a home inspector to make sure they can do the repairs needed.

The woman affected was standing next to him and he introduced us. We decided to meet at the local diner because we could not interview her at home. The interview went slow but she was calm and safe which was all that mattered. We had to sort out what medications she lost, make sure she had all her vital documents, and ask if we could assist her with sheltering for the night. Fortunately, she had relatives in town to help her get back on her feet. She was a red-haired, middle-aged professor with a strong look about her. I wondered what it would be like to be her or one of her students. My professors had become more than just instructors, but also great mentors and career coaches. I jumped in with psychological first aid and my partner approved of it before the meeting, a tool I was trained to use in this situation.

"How are you?" I said my words to match her pace and mirrored her body language to help her feel more comfortable.

"I have been through worse." I figured as much. We were taught that reactions to disasters can vary. For some people, it is the most traumatic event of their lives. For others, they could more easily endure the adversity. She seemed of the latter. "I think the worst part about this is that I lost my books. Those meant so much to me." One could look at her situation and consider her lucky. As a student, my heart and spirit broke for her. It's like a metaphor for losing one's repertoire of knowledge, of their world and themselves. I held back tears as she described her plans to regain her collection somehow.

The interview ended with the opportunity for her to reach out to us if she forgot anything we could help her with from the emergency. It felt better to hand her relief funds and my mood lifted slightly. At least she could buy food and get new clothes to recover. Our overarching mission as a nonprofit was to get people as close as we could back to where they were before a disaster. Serving the organization was fulfilling and became a healthy addiction for me. I wanted to be on call whenever my time permitted.

The first day of the spring semester hit hard. I was excited my girlfriends were all back but disheartened by the previous week's events and the looming thought of completing my studies. Leslie, Michelle, and I had lunch together. After I finished my class at 1 pm, I went to my internship which was only 2 pm-6 pm 3 days a week.

I arrived at the Fed and was so excited to learn about government financial regulations. The duties were intriguing but nothing like the employees who got to meet with the board of governors in DC every year. However, I resolved to put my head down in hopes of getting a job offer upon finishing the program. There were only 3 interns chosen that year and we were assigned to separate programs. This prevented us from fraternizing, so I wasn't fortunate enough to meet new friends from the program.

My first day went as expected and most of it was spent touring the beautiful facility. I felt so privileged and embarrassingly self-important. Although it is not technically a government agency, it is a regulatory entity that acts on its behalf. While many Americans think politicians are the most powerful citizens, scholars and academics knew better that it was the banking institutions.

It's ironic how boring partying as a regular hobby becomes when you find more life-enriching activities. I found working a nice escape from the everyday university life that I was comfortable with but bored in. Finally, I had direction beyond partying and getting laid. While partying and sex aren't fundamentally bad, I knew my execution was malignant to others and myself. Self-development was essential for me to make good decisions and feel fulfilled.

Although I was slowly shedding bad chemical habits and was smoking far less than before, I still yearned to hook up. I was in my room listening to music and relaxing that night when Carson texted me.

Carson Hey babe. You've seemed kind of distant. Everything ok?

Me: We've been dating for almost 8 months and you won't introduce me to your family. I'm Latina. How can I take you seriously?

Carson: I can't because you smoke.

Me: I'm slowing down and can take every precaution, change my clothes. Whatever.

Carson: No, it won't work.

Texting him was pissing me off so I set my phone down and let out a dramatic sigh. I knew he was lying so I called him out and instead of ghosting him, I cut him off.

Me: I need time to see other people… like see see other people.

Carson: So, we're breaking up? Over text?

Me: I don't have time to see you between my internship, volunteering, and school. I know this is sudden and I'm sorry but yes for now we're breaking up. If we're both single in the future and become more compatible, maybe we can come back together. Otherwise, I need to work on myself, and we haven't even been faithful to each other anyway.

Carson: Sorry Arie.

I stared at my phone for a minute. It was the right decision because I knew we could never give each other what the other wanted. I texted Vlad and Natasha.

Me: I broke up with him.

Natasha: YAY!!!! :D

Vlad: Oh bro…I'm sorry but you know you're better off. Run free little Arie!

The group text messages made me laugh through my grief. I hated confrontation and something about breaking up made me feel like a failure in so many ways. It felt like my intuition, heart, and soul were all wrong. Also, I despised that I was a failure at making relationships work. I was unnecessarily hard on myself because society makes it seem that being single is a miserable existence. I detested what other people thought and perceived about it. At least I had true friends by my side. Then I received another text.

Kathy: Hey man.

Me: KATHY! OMG girl I missed you. Happy New Year!

Kathy: You too. Angie told me you quit smoking cigarettes. Is that true? If so congrats.

Me: Not fully, but much less. Yeah, she probably noticed I stopped going outside as often.

Kathy: Want to come over and smoke a blunt?

Me: Absolutely.

My heart was filled again. My platonic friends meant as much if not more than my friends with benefits – they practically became family. The thought of being single didn't come back to my mind for a while and she didn't even realize what she did for me in that small, cordial gesture of an olive branch. It was only 8 pm so I drove over to her house, and we hung out like nothing had happened.

CHAPTER 13

Failure and Success

Martin was flirting with me again and was satisfied to hear that I was single. Deciding to put myself out there at least one more time before giving up, I invited him to celebrate Valentine's Day with me. I felt brave and simultaneously foolish-looking. He accepted the invitation. However, something was different about him and I couldn't put my finger on it, but it wasn't a good thing.

Aside from a lack of romance, despite my desire for it, everything was going well in my life. My volunteer work was getting noticed and I was able to win another scholarship towards my tuition. Why was I reverting? I had an easy modeling gig for a local boutique's website, and I didn't have a heavy course load. I was even considering doing another pageant for fun.

It was the second weekend of February. The months to graduation were diminishing. On a positive note, my inner romantic was excited and I cleaned up my room to make it presentable. I offered to host even though we could have gone out. My personality was becoming more introverted as my schedule filled up. Being around people grew tiring for me.

Before Martin arrived, I took a trip to the grocery

store and bought some typical ingredients. I made flounder, rice, and broccoli for dinner (since both of us were health conscious and liked seafood) and for dessert made chocolate fondue.

DWU students were lucky, our dorms had nice facilities and well-stocked kitchens on every floor for students to cook. I brought my ingredients in from the car and was delighted to see no one else was doing their Valentine's date in the building (or at least yet).

What commenced was utterly disappointing. He came over and brought a lovely bouquet of roses. For fun, I taught him how to salsa dance in our old school's Victorian Era-looking rec room. While we were dancing the food finished cooking in the oven and we ate right afterward. We even hooked up sensually. Then came the emotional disaster. I saw that he got a text from another woman asking when he would be at her house. Instead of causing a fuss, I pretended to grab a cigarette. The words that came out of his mouth next were expected. Again. AGAIN, WITH THIS BASTARD.

"Arie tonight was amazing…but I have to go. I forgot I have a commitment with another friend." He said apologetically. Wow… a repeat offense and under similar circumstances. My feelings didn't matter to him at all. He kissed me on the lips, and I let him. With a promise to text me later he left.

He ultimately texted me later – about two years, but it was too late. My attraction for him died with his third behavioral failure. Only a very select few men passed my test of time because out of sight or phone was out of mind. That night I decided to spend time with myself. I was not going to give up on finding someone amazing who accepted me as I am and wanted a relationship. That said, taking a break is routinely essential to have time for self-care. No more. At least for a long time, I was done.

I had been running more frequently with my boy schedule slowed down. I still had my DMU guys but that was it for now. I also slowly reduced the frequency we were hooking up due to being sore most of the time. Occasionally I just went over to smoke weed, do homework and play video games with them. By the end of the month, I was training for my first half marathon. It was exciting but destroyed my social schedule for the following four weeks.

Natasha was a competitive 5k runner and would take overall or youth women's placements at her races. Unlike myself, she was an elite runner but encouraged me to keep at it to help curb my cigarette addiction. We would run anywhere from 5 to 15 miles a week along with a couple of days reserved for strength training. For her, this was a cakewalk. She had already run a few full marathons. This at least made me confident in the advice she gave me. The running festival was in Dover on April 17th, the same week as my birthday. I was determined that my experience of 22 was going to be a turn for the better in both health and happiness!

My body was changing right before my eyes and I noticed it. We'd been training casually for at least 4 months before the official "season". The same distance run took a shorter amount of time. I could increase my speed throughout the run instead of slowing down. Pacing became instinctual as my muscle memory worked its magic. The visual transformation was not as dramatic because I was already slender, but my body began to sculpt. My appealing flat midsection slowly morphed into a set of solid abs. In the mirror, I saw the "princess" fall away and be pushed aside by my inner "warrior". I took pride in my natural knack for endurance-focused sports. My mind, body, emotions, and soul hardened.

This process helped me lessen my cigarette consumption, but resisting temptation was still challenging. Fortunately working out was incredible for my self-esteem. Who gives a flying fuck what other people think of me? Not to be an asshole, but for me, I got to the point where I looked around and didn't even compare myself to or want to look like anyone else. We all can do this; we simply must unapologetically be our non-fuck giving selves and do what we want. You compare yourself far less to others when you have almost everything if not everything you want. The strangest and most ironic part of my new regimen was that despite my lack of time, my sex drive went through the roof. It was sweet torture being both horny and confident without a sexy piece of ass to lay it down on.

The week before the race was our tapering time so with my schedule opened up, I made time to get my fix. My boys were busy but loyally there for me. It is as if the past couple of months flew by as I threw myself into better coping skills and habits. The cravings for their touch sunk in when I texted them.

Me: In the mood to play?
Anthony: Matt found out last week he got into

Harvard for his Ph.D. and the team has scouts visiting from the Marlins next week! YES. COME THRU.

I smiled to myself. Well, it looks like I wasn't the only one working on me. My pride welled up for them because I had seen them put in the work on countless occasions where I was over their place hanging out. Smoking blunts, cuddling, having sex, and studying made their apartment a hospitable environment for me over the year.

Me: I'll be over in an hourish.

Tomorrow was my birthday, and my race was closer than it felt. My visit didn't begin as it usually did, and the celebration was nourishing the atmosphere. It was only 2 in the afternoon, but Anthony started popping bottles. I don't recommend drinking or smoking before a race but to an extent, youth could offset my poor habits in athletic performances. I knew it wasn't a permanent trait, but something I relished about my circumstances.

"To Mattie, Me and Arie!" Anthony cheered as he, Matt, and I clinked solo cups full of champagne. I rolled a blunt as became customary and jumped on the couch rolling over on my back. They had a table they used for drinking games, so they racked up a pyramid of champagne on each side.

"I'm opting out. You guys play. I'll smoke and sip!" I waved my blunt around.

"Let's do it," Matt replied agreeably. They were so attractive, and I watched them while we discussed our big post-graduation plans. Matt wanted to get his

Ph.D. in Physics. Anthony was going to try to go pro in baseball and if not pursue a similar academic path. It was so inspiring to share friendships with such accomplished and insightful people. Plus, they were easy to look at. The thought made me grateful.

"You're glowing little one," Anthony spoke and laughed as he looked at me. My face relaxed but I was elated to spend more time with them. However, melancholy crept in with the thought of us all moving away. My expression changed. "Don't worry. I'm staying one more year for the second part of my master's program, so even if you head to Phili, NYC, or Baltimore you'll be close enough to see me."

"I'm glad to hear it. I still haven't gotten any offers from the Fed. I may try to stay in the area to live with Vlad and Tasha again." I informed him. The thought of living with my best friends again lifted my mood slightly. At least I could get one more year with him if I was lucky enough to stay in Wilmington. I loved being pocketed between all the big cities. Everything entertainment and fashion-wise were easily accessible.

"Well don't worry. If they don't take you. you'll find something in your major." Matt reassured me. My grades were high, and my internship was going well, along with their kindness I relaxed more. I'd still miss Mattie. My thoughts tumbled with the champagne bubbles, and I knew once Anthony left, I would feel devastated. It wasn't his fault. It was mine for being so damn emotional and getting attached when I agreed I wouldn't. Their presence was like a comfort object that soothed any boo-boos, scars, or scratches. They filled so many of my days with youthful exuberance and fantastical, dreamlike euphoria.

We drank and smoked more. The guys went back and forth on if they wanted to bet sexual favors on games. I discouraged it while laying on their couch with my shirt half up like a tease. We discussed the recent COD update and how annoying it was. Then Anthony pulled out the Nintendo 64.

"WHATTTTT?" I asked, stunned. "Oh, you guys have been holding out!" We commenced with Super Smash Bros, a classic for group playing. Most American kids in the millennial generation had a Super Smash Bros character they played routinely. The game was nostalgic and brought back so many childhood memories of spending time at my friends' homes. Anthony won 3 rounds, Matt won 4 and I won 2. Of course, we all played the same characters every match.

While playing we finished the second bottle of champagne, but it had been at least 2 hours since I got there. This helped me to avoid feeling sick and I was able to stay hydrated.

"Can you guys come to my race this weekend?" I asked hopefully.

"I can," Mattie said and looked at Anthony who agreed.

"We can probably get the boys together as your cheering section." Anthony looked back over to me and grinned. I loved the idea and encouraged it. Nothing could have changed that I felt like such a lucky girl. I had so much love and support that my heart felt gigantic. My chest felt full and hot. I put down my controller and took Anthony's controller from his hands to set them on the coffee table. I sat on Anthony's lap and gave him a big sloppy kiss. His hands moved down to my thighs, which turned me on. There was some time to play with my week's schedule being less intense.

Matt grabbed my hand and walked me into the bedroom. His best bro got up from the couch and followed. Of course, I was going to savor each feel and thrust I could before we all had to depart. The experience of having them with the knowledge I'd be losing them made the session painfully beautiful. I tried to visually capture everything in my memory and perspective so that I could lock them away for me to remember forever. Anthony's soft blue eyes, Mattie's deep dark brown ones that matched mine exactly. Their souls were muddled and lost like mine, but we were all sexually tense, stressed-out overachievers.

Everything was how we all wanted it to be. There was never a lack of consent among the group, and I never did feel pressure to put out if I wasn't in the mood. They were a cheerful pair apart of a jovial group that was easy for my friends and I to get along with.

We spent some time after the gentler session cuddling. Matt had to tap out early to get back to studying. Anthony and I took a nap. I woke up and it was 7 pm. I kissed the boys goodbye and headed back to my dorms. The rest of the week I ran a couple more times to prepare for the race.

On my first half marathon race day I was apprehensive not knowing how my previous weekend's drinking would impact everything. Equally, I was excited to pursue a new goal that I was measurably improving at.

On the morning of the running festival, we had perfect weather. It was a cool 57 degrees which was a good thing to prevent overheating. I slept over at Natasha's the night before so she, Vlad, and I could drive to the festival together.

We decided to pack and eat light. I chose a banana and hard-boiled egg to fuel up for the day. She estimated with my current speed at 10 minutes per mile I could pull a 2:16:50 time. Watching the marathon runners stretch was intimidating. I couldn't fathom what training for 26.2 miles was like and was concerned just for my half-marathon. Natasha and I adjusted our gear.

The start was about to commence and the 5k group moved to the front, followed by half marathon runners who were followed by the marathon runners. I was toward the back of the half marathon group so I could see some of the elite marathon runners through the holes in the crowd. The energy was present among the runners and the air above us. It felt incredible to be surrounded by that many people who shared the same interest.

The announcer gave each pace group their permission to go and we were off. Vlad agreed to meet us at the finish line and said he didn't mind waiting with his friend Steve. Tasha and I trotted along the course energetically. The first couple of miles felt like being a part of a herd of cattle. Runners were all squished in their respective pace groups.

Getting through the next few miles after that was much better as the crowds dissipated. My breathing and our pace were both steady. I started to feel thirsty but resisted my urge to drink since I failed to keep water down without it hurting my stomach on training runs.

At mile 10 the guys were waiting with a big megaphone cheering and heckling the runners. I could hear them before I saw them. I was thrilled to see Anthony having fun with his crew and watching the event. Kristian was holding a cowbell and saw me. He then pointed me out to the group who started cheering madly. I sprinted over to Anthony, Matt, and Kristian to get a group hug.

They were all shirtless which I took immediate notice of and cracked up while they squeezed me. The next three miles were so difficult, so their cheers were needed to finish the damn race. I ran off and waved them goodbye sprinting to catch back up to Natasha. She promised beforehand to keep me on pace so that I could finish within my goal time.

My calves were aching and despite the slight wind, I was sweating. I expressed doubts and a desire to walk. Natasha relented, coaching me to keep going and push past the pain. We hit a few more water stops and kept the same distance from the pace group behind us for most of the race. Seeing the mile 12 sign was recharging and we powered through the last 1.1 miles. The view of the finish line and clock was a great relief. The race clock showed a time of 2:12:54 when we approached. The announcer was calling out racers' names and we ran through holding hands. I limped over slowly but joyfully to the volunteers handing out water, sports drink mix, snacks and finisher medals. There was a stage where winners of the half marathon and 5k were already celebrating. I couldn't help but consider how talented and inspiring these elite athletes were.

We met up with Vlad and Steve outside of the runners' area. They were so proud of us and gave us slices of pizza out of a box they grabbed during the race. Afterward, we went to their apartment and celebrated with our group of shared friends. There was no hooking up on my or Natasha's behalf because we were both sore from the athletic effort. I didn't even feel a need to smoke as my endorphins were pumping through my veins. Regardless, we did enjoy ample joints of weed.

The race was on a Saturday, so I at least had Sunday to recover. I woke up the next morning in my dorm feeling like crap. My desk was messy but on top of my stack of women's studies homework was my medal. With the minimal energy I had, I reached over and put it on. "What a week." I thought to myself. I was exhausted but limped over to the dining hall for some coffee. It was an easy way to get a recovery walk in.

I finished the weekend off in solitude and stayed in to rest. My homework was mostly done so I completed it that afternoon.

Me: Thank you guys so much. That meant the world to me.
Kristian: You're welcome. ☺
Anthony: CONGRATULATIONS!
Matt: Great job and you're welcome!

What I would give to go back and see some of our Facebook messages or texts. Despite not being my official or monogamous "boyfriends", my boy team seldom disappointed and never disrespected me. The next week was boring, and I felt physically repaired by Wednesday. As May approached, I sank into a post-race blues and depressive state. Even though the guys promised continued communication, I felt like graduation was a type of breakup for us. We all had to eventually move on, grow up and find out who we were.

CHAPTER 14

Bittersweet Greetings and Farewells

L ooking at my phone I grimaced and groaned to myself. Seeing the date gave me anxiety. It was the last day of April. It would only be one more month until my life and social circle would change drastically. My phone showed that it was Sunday and I decided to go on a run. I didn't have much homework and was feeling better from the previous week of race recovery.

The weather was warming up and the thermometer on my laptop read 62 degrees. My thoughts ran at a faster pace than my legs. Spring was in full bloom and the city was bursting with a panorama of colors. Tulips peeked out of a corner pot at the Hott Chocolate Café where Madison was still working. She was one of my luckier friends who already was hired for a post-graduation job months before graduation. As a talented writer and English major, she was hired almost immediately in a teaching position.

I pondered about my job prospects. While I was given a 100/100 on my internship rating from my employer and professor, my supervisor informed me that there were only entry-level and mid-level openings in the Baltimore and DC regions. Although it could seem like an unwise decision, I didn't want to move from my social circle during my first year of real adulthood. Fortunately, I had a job offer as a full-time junior accountant. It wasn't glamorous but it was a good backup to get into finance or accounting.

DRO still had volunteer opportunities but no paid positions that I was qualified for. I didn't let that discourage me from serving the organization as it was such a life enriching activity. Vlad and Natasha were thrilled to have me move in again which was a positive thing I had going for me. It was thrilling to consider the fun we'd still have years after university. Natasha was getting ready to graduate with a math degree. We mutually agreed upon a shared graduation party with our friends. So much was changing in a four-week window, and I was overwhelmed.

Getting back from my run I was happy to see a text from Kathy.

Kathy: Hey man, you good to hang out?
Me: Yeah dude!
Kathy: Sweet, I'll be up at campus in 45 minutes!

She picked me up and we drove back to her house. Deedee was there and I freaked out. I greeted her with a huge hug. She and Angie had long broken up but remained friends. Knowing both, it wouldn't be long until they ended up back together. It wasn't too upsetting of news to hear. The mood and energy were just as they were almost two years ago when we were carelessly riding around in Kathy's jeep.

Something about her had changed. She had gotten

into a traumatic accident with her Jeep a few months prior and narrowly missed death. Another car hit her at a cross section and her car flipped over. In that accident, she lost a few pipes but also avoided getting a citation for weed. Left physically fine, she might have changed emotionally from the traumatic event. I worried if she would remain friends with me after graduation and for good reason with her ghosting me before the accident. It would have helped to know how she was feeling, but when I asked about it, she didn't open up. I had no idea what she was going through but desired to.

We resolved to burn our index cards from the past 4 years at a bonfire the next weekend. This would also be my second to last time with my two female friends in one room. I loved my friends. They were my everything. They were family away from family and Kathy knew I had a little girl crush on her but didn't dare to act on anything.

"What are your guys' plans after school?" I asked them and toked on the joint Kathy handed me.

"I'm going to work for this pre-school I've been at part-time. They're upping me to full-time!" Deedee sounded ecstatic about spending more time with her kiddos. She loved her job and was an early childhood education major, so it fit perfectly into her career plans. Kathy looked a little annoyed and fidgeted with the ponytail holder on her wrist.

"I don't even know man." She said, sounding hopeless.

"Don't worry dude. Whatever you go for, you're going to kill it!" I encouraged her gently. We digressed from the topic and moved on to discussing popular girls at DWU and other schools' students we considered sexy. It surprised me that Kathy wasn't jumping at the opportunity for grad school or to work in a lab. She majored in chemistry and seemed to have good grades. Her parents were fully supportive of her and not influential in what career she pursued. I sometimes envied her for having them. We finished smoking and I headed back to school.

The next week dragged on and flew by concurrently. Time moved randomly and some moments felt faster than others. Part of my mind fantasized about living in this world forever. For some students, grad school was a way to partially extend it, but my career didn't require it upfront. I dreaded the looming loss of some of my friends.

On Saturday night I went to Kathy's for our "knowledge bonfire". With my index cards from the past four years packed in my backpack, I got in my car and drove to the gas station for blunt wraps first and then to Kathy's. Upon arrival at her house, I was greeted by her mom. My blonde bombshell buddy was in her room tending to her cannabis plant. We greeted each other with a hug, and I sat down to begin rolling. Deedee arrived shortly after. To kick off the night we laid the cards down on the floor and took photos of them with our phones.

Kathy finished up tending to her "green baby" and we followed her downstairs after our mini photoshoot. The night was young, and I decided to stay 4-5 hours so that if I drank a beer and lots of water, I would be ok to drive back to campus. We popped open 3 beers and toasted to a successful academic year. Music flowed around us from Deedee's wireless speaker, and we started the fire on top of a fire pit in Kathy's fenced-in backyard. The sun was setting so the sky was beginning to darken. Shadows from the few trees cast around us.

One by one we disposed of our index cards. S'mores were crafted, and old jokes and promises that weren't kept were made. Unforgettable is how I would describe that night. The beer gave me a slight buzz for a couple of hours, but I was back to my normal self again. Both Kathy and Deedee looked glorious under the starry sky with the dim light of the fire caressing their faces. One moment in time can last in your memory for a lifetime if it matters enough to you. I looked down at myself. Wearing my signature bow in my hair, flip flops, a pink DWU hoodie, two braids, and daisy duke shorts, I was a typical college chick. I loved it and the atmosphere I was living in at that moment.

That evening was the last night I saw those two together. It still haunts me to this day that something as fragile as academic phases ending can sever relationships. Why is life designed so that we cannot repeat the past? Pictures and videos don't do the greatest experiences justice. My drive home was pleasant, but I foresaw what was happening.

Of course, Michelle and Leslie wanted a last hurrah despite them not being the ones graduating. Though I assured them it wouldn't be the last they saw of me. We decided to spend it one last time with the guys. Before finals, the frats were all throwing end-of-year parties for the seniors to pass the torch to the juniors. My heart felt more tender with each approaching day, and I was abnormally emotional over everything. I was halfway back to my previous amount of cigarette smoking and disappointed with my habitual self-medicating.

I woke up on May 14th heartbroken and feeling the same way I did when I got dumped by Calvin. Most students and parents of students were so excited about the upcoming ceremonies, but I was distraught. In-person classes ended the day before, so we had an entire week to study for finals. I drew further and further into my mind. Overthinking became a new toxic hobby of mine, but I was determined to have an amazing night with my girls and boys. *One last time*. I shook at the consideration. No one saw through my smile those days to see the demolished girl inside, and I kept up a decent act.

At least the party that night was something my aching soul was craving as a reprieve from the anxiety. On this day I went to Michelle's room as a subtle way to pass my legacy down to the next class. She and Leslie glowed as all three of us admired ourselves in her and her suitemate's bathroom hall mirror. My choice for a hair accessory was a black bow, a nod at my melodramatic grief. I looked decent but couldn't look at myself for longer than a glance. My soul was tired and crushed. I forced a smile and creased my eyes to make it believable. All these greetings and farewells culminated in a strange theory. I felt these people could all have been my platonic or romantic soulmates. It felt like they were meant to be in my life by some unexplainable fate.

I didn't want to drink that night since I was the driver, but I wanted to show my appreciation for the boys. Before heading to DMU's frat row, we hit the liquor store and I hurried in. The girls waited in the car, and I purchased top-shelf champagne. It was going to be a night of bonding and celebration.

Their frat house was lit up and every window had people in it. It was like an urban piece of artwork. I wondered if anyone else was hiding their pain. Was the possibility of career success that much more fascinating than the people we came to know on the way there? I didn't know anymore. My head was spinning but I kept my composure. Kristian once again greeted us at the door – I kissed him on the cheek, and he playfully spanked me. We walked in where Jake, Nate, Andy, and Anthony were congregating in the entryway around some of their brothers. Matt was in the kitchen grabbing himself a beer but walked out to see us. I gave Anthony the champagne, he then thanked me and popped the cork off. My hugs were tighter and lasted longer than usual.

There were more people at this party than the others I attended that semester. Almost all the 40 brothers and their friends were present. The house was stuffed to the brim with humans and the scent of stale beer – an aroma that had grown on me over time. We followed the boys into the living room to play beer pong and danced on the sidelines while the four played. Dancing next to each of them on their off turn became a game. One of my favorite songs came on and I began to sing. The booze-soaked brothers amused me, and a couple started laughing at me and dancing back when I got to them. They thought it was adorable and comedic.

Michelle and Leslie jumped in and joined their favorite hook up buddy in some playful dancing. I had three joints already rolled in my cigarette box and I pulled them out to share in a rotation. Matt and Anthony regretfully declined as they both had impending drug tests to worry about. The song ended and we were all losing it with hilarity.

The guys pulled out all the comforting stops and prepared a hookah for us. The environment was so lively, and we were lucky to find a place to party that rarely had fighting or severe drug issues. I drank a solo cup of champagne Anthony poured for me and changed my plans to get drunk since I could walk to their apartment from the party. Leslie and Michelle were fine with ending the night at the house. A duck ran past us and we all watched as a freshman rush member tried to chase it around. As a hazing act, the freshman had to raise and butcher a duck each for the upperclassmen to gain entry as a brother into the allusive and exclusive fraternity house.

We went to the basement to jam out in the strobe lights and get close to each other. Matt had been dancing with a new girl I hadn't met, so I let him get his game on. Anthony and I paired up. Dancing with him was so fun and for a white boy, he could impressively keep up with my Boricua style of movement. Swaying around in the flashing beams it felt like time passed in slow motion. Then a slower rap song came on. We stayed on the floor and our movement felt like a creatively romantic farewell. It was both to our regular relationship and our current lifestyle. He felt as I did and hid it well, especially since he had one more year at DMU for his program.

Through the flashes, my mind was carried away to

an excruciating place. Without making a sound, my face began to feel wet, and tears dripped down my cheeks. I gazed hopelessly into his eyes. I loved him so much.

"Arie…" Anthony spoke quietly so that no one could hear. He tried to go on, but I let go of his hands and walked away from the dance floor wiping my tears to quickly gather myself. My emotions were brittle. He followed me. "Let's go outside on top of the house for some privacy. Want to grab a smoke together?" I nodded and sniffed. We walked up the stairs to the first floor and walked up the four floors of stairs on the opposite side of the house to the roof. Nobody was up there so we could get some alone time.

"This…" my eyes started watering as I attempted to speak. "This just…hurts."

"Oh, please. At least we'll be together this summer and hopefully, we can hang out next year too when I'm in semester." His words meant so much to me. I lit my cigarette and stifled my feelings as much as I could. "It's ok to feel sad but just try to look on the bright side, little one." I closed the few feet of distance between us and hugged him. I turned around and leaned on him.

"Eventually when you and I separate…I think I'm going to be heartbroken." I confided.

"Really?" He sounded somewhat surprised and searched for more reassuring words. "No matter what our future circumstances I will at least always try to keep you in my life as a friend."

"I hope so." I expressed.

He kissed me softly. We finished smoking and headed back downstairs to enjoy the party. Kristian was a junior, so I also was happy I'd get to see him over the next year too. I felt spoiled to get another year with at least two of them. The festivities were still roaring, and a keg was brought out for party-goers to do keg stands. By this point in my college "career", I've seen countless done but never participated. I expressed this to Anthony who pulled Kristian from the door. He closed and locked it before following Anthony back with me.

Their hands were warm on my thighs, and they tilted me over into a handstand above the keg. The brothers in the room hooted and hollered like a pack of unruly coyotes. Jake turned up the keg lever to let it rip and I was immediately sprayed with a splash of beer while choking on it. Anthony and Kristian lowered me down and were fairly laughing at me. I was a sloppy hot mess but even I found stress relieving humor in it all.

I went to the bathroom to wipe my face off and rejoined Anthony. We went to hang out with his clique in Nate's room. Leslie sat on his lap, and Michelle sat right next to Jake. I occupied Anthony's lap with my butt on the couch and my legs on him. The night was young and beautiful like the group of my friends. Seeing them together in one room the last time felt surreal. My cell phone showed that the time was 11:11. I made a wish that I could keep all my friends. Although it was unrealistic, I hoped it would work. We spent the next couple of hours drinking, talking, and toking. Some of their frat bros did end up doing lines of coke but were careful not to overdo it. None of us ladies partook as we preferred the green. Instead of coke, Anthony micro dosed a couple of mushrooms. He offered me some, but I declined as I feared my possible reaction to them.

Around 1:30 in the morning we headed to Matt and

Anthony's place. Matt went to the girl's sorority, and I was sad that he didn't follow us. However, as his friend, it was silly for me to be jealous, and I wanted him to enjoy the night. Michelle and Leslie retreated with their boys. I walked outside with Anthony and kissed Kristian on the way out. After a small complaint about my heels, Anthony offered a piggyback ride. I was in shorts, so I didn't care and hopped on his back. We only lasted a block because I was drunk and wanted to get down to smoke a cigarette on the way.

I asked if he wanted to take a walk before going to his place and he obliged. We walked along the moonlit sidewalk together. We exchanged secrets among the trees, flowers, and city sidewalks. I told him some of my most profound feelings and he traded his. Life can feel flawless at times, especially when we're seeing someone without their mask. He delved into information about his family, and I gave him the pleasure of learning about mine. In another world, with a more compatible set of values, we could have been something long-term. Those 20 minutes felt like a walk in that alternate universe. We turned around and went to his apartment.

The sex was more compassionate and connected. It was more akin to tender lovemaking than the passionate flame combustion that was our normal routine. I won't deny that I soaked the energy in. We glanced into each other's eyes, and both looked down at our bodies to watch the slow and sexy movements. After he gave me a back rub and I returned the favor. I was light enough to walk on his back and he recommended I do it. Before going to bed we snuggled up on the living room couch with some water and two joints. He was so calming and any girl he could land was lucky to be with him. I also learned that he was a compatible zodiac sign for me as either a friend, lover, or both. Funny coincidence. We laughed at our opposite interests, his of astronomy, actual space, and my love for astrology.

After that cute moment, we returned to the bedroom and whispered a few more sweet nothings to each other. We were both dwindling in energy reserves but still desiring to live in the night. The next morning, we woke, and for the first time in months, our high-achieving selves slept in, with each other. His body was so warm and comfortable for me. While he was fit and attractive, he and his body had become so familiar which was distinctive. I never told him that I loved him which I regret. I gently brushed his hair back with my hand and kissed his cheeks a few times. His eyes opened slowly, and I kissed his lips as they curled into a smile.

We kanoodled in bed for a few more minutes and I got up to make coffee. What a perfect last weekend, both fun and intimate. He ate breakfast as we drank coffee together. I was waiting to eat breakfast or lunch at DWU with my girlfriends after I picked them up and dropped them off. Matt got back before I left, greeted us politely but went straight to bed. The jealousy pierced through my emotions again, but I let him sleep peacefully and said nothing negative. I looked at the clock and saw it was 10:45 am.

Leslie had just texted ten minutes earlier, but I didn't hear it. I texted her and Michelle back. They had a wonderful time but needed to be picked up. I gave Anthony one last kiss, pulled up my shorts over my red and black thong, and went to grab the girls. As usual, we skipped breakfast to sleep more and met for lunch. I pined and wished during that nap that I could just live in a dream state like that weekend forever. That was a silly fantasy but valid with the way I was feeling towards the loss of an old life stage and the beginning of a new one.

CHAPTER 15

Graduation

The last week of May had finally crashed unwelcomed into my life. How dare it. It was finals for most surrounding universities and our own. The week prior most students did not go out and spent the entire week studying as the time was meant to be used. I did not sacrifice bud since it seemed to help me relax for long study sessions and actual exam days. Maturely, I did lay off the alcohol and partying to keep my memory capabilities boosted. I still didn't find another job offer aside from the junior accountant job but was thankful I had something lined up.

It hit me that I needed to pack before it was too late. The move wouldn't be terrible, and I estimated it would only take two to three car rides with my car from the school to Vlad and Tasha's. Packing was a tough task to begin and execute, not just because it was a pain, but it was additionally depressing. I wanted this experience to last forever, but I knew it couldn't. I would have to find my thrills in more mature hobbies and move on with my career. Even if I did stay in grad school, the schedule is far denser so it's not like students party like they do in undergrad. I acknowledged to myself that at least I got to experience an amazing coming of age with these gorgeous people.

Each day my dorm room lost a decoration or two as they were packed away for the move. My family was coming to watch my graduation but that was the last thing on my mind. I'd have so much more time with my family than with my college friends. It was raining for half of the week which felt appropriate for my grief. I grouped up with a few classmates for one of my courses and met a couple of days that week to study. It felt like I was being kicked out of a parent's house. I tried to use my coping skills and ran a few days that week to break up my mundane schedule. The sessions helped me meditate on the future and destress. At least something healthy kept me sane those days.

Going into finals I felt prepared, but emotionally I was not prepared to leave DWU. With each exam, I threw away the last of each stack of index note cards that I did not burn at Kathy's celebration. Our finals were challenging, and some exams could last up to 2-3 hours. I persevered and finished up with high scores. My overall grades reflected the hard work I put in when no one was watching except occasional study group members and my suitemate.

The guys and I stayed in touch through the week as they also completed their finals. Everyone had a week after their exams ended to pack up and move out. We had until 7 days after the last possible day of finals. To my dismay, I could only find time to see Jake one more time during the day to smoke. Despite my absence, the others understood my sincere wishes for them. Kristian and Anthony knew they would see me again soon anyway, so they were consumed by their studies.

Graduation was the day before the move-out day on

May 28th. I spent the days after finals moving my stuff from my dorm to Vlad and Natasha's. The Wednesday before graduation day I was almost done. Scanning my room, I had packed or moved everything I didn't need over the next few days. I stood on my desk to get a view over the tree line, because why the hell not? The view was stunning in a maze of city sky twists and turns.

I didn't have any other plans for the day, so I went back to my new apartment to smoke with my familiar roomies. I needed to not get sucked into too much introspection as it only increased my instability. At least I had cut most of my cigarette smoking out and was down to three a day.

My parents and extended family arrived from out of state the next morning. I visited them at the hotel they were staying at. They were coming to our school's church ceremony on Friday and then the graduation ceremony on Saturday. Our shared meals together were pleasant, and we discussed a variety of topics over Italian food. We also talked about my plans to visit them over the summer. I had neglected to visit them being so busy with school, so I remained positive about it.

The next day was an out-of-body experience for me. The agenda started and we rehearsed for graduation at the convention center that morning. I waved at Kathy who half-heartedly waved back from the science department area. I sensed a similar disappointment in her, but she looked more in shock. That afternoon we had the school church ceremony. DWU was founded as a Catholic all-women's convent and university. We were lucky we weren't required to go to church like I had to previously do over a decade before in elementary and middle school.

My family was so excited for me, and I appreciated their support. The travel was a pain, so I knew they loved me a lot to make it through the graduation traffic with all the surrounding schools. That evening after dinner they retreated to their hotel rooms. They were all staying in the same hotel near my school so they could walk to the convention center. I thanked my mother, and she gave me a graduation gift to open early before I left the hotel. Opening it I was surprised to see my great grandmother's sapphire and platinum flower ring that she gifted to my mother for graduating high school. Immediately, I tried it on to check how it fit and it was a little big on me.

"This was given to me for my graduation. Your generation lives on a foreign planet compared to mine but maybe it can serve you and bring you some luck." I shed a few tears and hugged her. "You can size it down if you need to since it's yours now. I love you Arie-Marie". I was a proud fourth-generationer astrology gal. My mother, great aunt, great grandmother, and I were all of the same zodiac sign. We shared similar fiery personalities and a hunger for accomplishing big things for the family. She walked out to the car with me and waved as I drove away.

That night I took the time to walk the campus and its buildings alone. Most of them were open at odd hours to students who wanted to study in the middle of the night for finals or midterms. I walked to the opposite side of the campus from the upperclassmen dorms and started in the science building. Already things changed so much since I starting going there. In my sophomore year, the school became a university and before that, it was only a college. The name change upped its prestige among academics. More construction projects began as the campus was expanding.

There was a new addition to the building that had a glass hallway leading to a terrace. I walked to it and appreciated the view. Next was the freshman and sophomore dorms which also housed the dining hall. This place hosted my early shenanigans and taught me how to be comfortable with who I was.

The music hall and theater were always a treat to walk around. Remembering how crazy my piano practice schedule was for pageants made me smile and shake my head. Connected to the school's gym and other academic buildings, it was central on campus. The gym housed a basketball court, workout room with equipment, a dance studio, and three racquetball courts. It all felt so homey. Lastly, I finished with a final tour of the IT building, the academic halls, and my dorm building. What an unbelievable trip. This place was a social paradise in my unwitting mind.

I went to bed and woke up too early the next morning. After showering I went to the dining hall in sweats for some coffee. I returned to my dorm with a full 16 oz. disposable cup so I could keep drinking it to wake up. Putting on my semi-formal black party dress I checked out my body in the mirror. The dress fit elegantly and showed off my figure but not in a culturally disrespectful way my family would disapprove of.

I put my hair up in rollers and had ample time before I needed to meet my family for brunch. I took my time doing my makeup and played some music. Since my suitemate was moving out that day and was also a senior, I knew it'd be the last time I'd see her in person. We said our goodbyes and hugged each other. In my final hours as a college student, I smoked a blunt and got ready.

I was on time to meet my family and got to the restaurant at the same time as them. We agreed the evening before to meet a couple of hours before the start of the ceremony at a restaurant nearby. My mother was thoughtful and made reservations in advance. She also planned a small and private graduation party at a local Italian restaurant. The meal was pleasant and after we walked to where the ceremony was held. When entering the building, I left my loved ones. My family knew I couldn't meet with them until after everything was over because I had to find my spot.

In the sea of blue robes, I saw familiar faces and said hello to professors and friends. Kathy also made an appearance nearby. I walked up to her and hugged her. She nervously greeted me and said she had to find her spot. That was the last time I ever saw her in person and it's still something I will never understand. She ended up staying in the area but distanced herself from me aside from an annual or biannual text. If she came back to me now as a friend, I'd still accept her.

Teachers and students found their spots in line while everyone had to wait for the commencement music to start which was the audio cue to march in. Everyone was finally seated, and the music blasted out to the hall. We walked in, took our seats and the speeches began. The school had a compelling alumna speak on her experience as an oil company negotiator for a US-owned firm and how she navigated working in a middle east warzone. It was inspiring and served its purpose to impress the huge crowd of graduates and their families.

The announcer stated that the ceremony was wrapping up and that graduates would now be handed their diplomas. One by one we were called and shook hands with the university president. It was my turn and my family screamed above the average clapping. The ceremony finally ended, and students marched out. I waited for my family apprehensively in the hall. I felt mentally scattered and was so confused at how I could keep successfully masking my emotions.

My family met up with me for my dinner party which Vlad and Tasha also attended. Tasha's graduation wasn't until the next day, so she was able to make it. Then after that we would hold our mutual party for our friend group. I ended up attending her ceremony and going to her family's party with her. It went by quickly, and I confided in my mother as I waved the rest of my family goodbye. She told me that I could do anything, and she was so proud of me. This helped me feel a little better, but I knew the real key was mentally, physically, spiritually, and emotionally detaching from this life phase.

She and my stepdad departed when I resolved to gather everything left in my dorm. Graduates were allowed to spend that night in the dorm buildings, but I didn't want to. It was eerily empty as most students including current ones moved out early. With a heavy heart, I packed away my last things, looked at both mirrors, and observed what was going on outside my window for a minute. It took a few trips to load the remainder of my belongings into my car, but I was able to manage alone.

Finally, I dropped my key off with the floor RA, hugged her, and left the dorm building. The door closed behind me and I felt more sadness coming on, but I resisted getting emotional. There was no need because I was blessed with a great family, a consistent group of friends, good health, an apartment, some "cool" hobbies, and a job lined up. I stepped out of my old life and timidly, but optimistically entered my new one.